WITHDRAWN

THE FRENZY

Also by Francesca Lia Block:

The
FRENZY

FRANCESCA LIA BLOCK

HARPER TEEN

An Imprint of HarperCollinsPublishers

HarperTeen is an imprint of HarperCollins Publishers.

The Frenzy
Copyright © 2010 by Francesca Lia Block
All rights reserved. Printed in the United States of America.
www.harperteen.com
——
Library of Congress Cataloging-in-Publication Data
Block, Francesca Lia.
The frenzy / Francesca Lia Block. — 1st ed.
p. cm.
Summary: When she was thirteen, something terrifying and mysterious
happened to Liv that she still does not understand, and now, four years
later, her dark secret threatens to tear her apart from her family and her
true love.
ISBN 978-0-06-192666-2
[1. Shapeshifting—Fiction. 2. Identity—Fiction. 3. Love—Fiction.
4. Supernatural—Fiction. 5. Werewolves—Fiction. 6. Family problems—
Fiction.] I. Title.
PZ7.B61945Fr 2010   2009053453
[Fic]—dc22   CIP
                                                                       AC
——
Typography by Alison Klapthor
10   11   12   13   14   CG/RRDB   10   9   8   7   6   5   4   3   2   1
❖
First Edition

For J.K. and for A.L.M.

Acknowledgments

Sera Gamble suggested I take on the story of a female werewolf. Carmen Staton provided excellent werewolf research. My thanks go to my agent, Lydia Wills; my editor, Tara Weikum; and Jocelyn Davies, Laura Kaplan, Susan Katz, and everyone at Harper, as always, for supporting me and making everything possible. I would also like to thank Charlie Blakemore for his suggestions. Finally, I am grateful to Gilda Block for reading this aloud to me as I was recovering from eye surgery so that I could make the final changes to Liv's story, and to my children for everything they are.

Liv

At some point in everyone's life they ask the question, "Who am I?"

Four years ago when I turned thirteen I asked the question, "What am I?"

I had changed.

But I didn't know how or why, or what I had become.

It was my thirteenth birthday. I woke early in my lavender canopy bed, with a tight, painful feeling in my abdomen, and went to the bathroom. There was a stain on my white cotton, lace-trimmed underwear. My face in the mirror was paler than usual, making my eyes glitter a poison green, and I suddenly felt ashamed of the telling, bright red color of my hair. I had never minded it before. Outside of our three-story Colonial house snow fell over the winter garden, where lilies waited under the earth, and I imagined my blood staining all that whiteness.

I washed and used the pads my mother had given me, got dressed and went downstairs. I smelled the sausages my parents had cooked for breakfast before they went out hunting deer and my stomach cramped again, this time with hunger, but I had vowed to be a vegetarian starting on this day. I'd seen a show about the cruel conditions livestock were exposed to. And I thought maybe if I didn't eat blood, I'd keep the blood from flowing out of my body. So even though I craved red meat I ate cornflakes and milk instead.

We were going to have a party and a few girls from my school had been invited but none of them could come. They said it was because they were busy with early holiday parties. But I knew it was because they didn't like me that much. I mostly kept to myself. I'd never really had any girlfriends, anyway, except for Sadie Nelson. Sadie had suddenly lost a lot of weight and been accepted by a group of girls who thought they were too cool for me. I had been okay with the other girls not coming to my party, but the fact that Sadie wasn't going to be there made me inconsolable. So my mom tried to cheer me up by serving a special lunch for Mr. and Mrs. McIntyre and their son, Pace. Pace was the only real friend I had then. He had promised to make me a new music mix as a present. We'd sit up in my room, eat cupcakes and talk about boys.

But as it turned out, I didn't have a party that year at all.

When I saw my mother's truck coming up the snowy driveway I ran out of the house. I wanted to tell her about my period. She called it "the curse" but she said it with an almost gleeful smile.

I am usually a mess and my mother is an ex–beauty queen whose hair and makeup are always perfect, even when she's hunting deer in the woods. You would never know we are mother and daughter. That day she looked perfect as usual with her sleek chestnut brown hair in a high ponytail, her pink lipstick neatly applied and her bright orange down jacket. She was in the truck with my father and her hunting dog, Scoot. My parents had met in high school—he was the quarterback and she was the student body president—but they didn't have much of a relationship anymore. They rarely went anywhere together or even spoke much to each other except to complain, but that morning they were talking in an animated way. Their voices made me pause. My ears perked and my vision seemed to become more focused.

That was when I saw the wolf bleeding through the bag in the back of the truck.

I was only a thirteen-year-old girl with a temper

but when I saw the bloody wolf in the back of my mother's truck I seethed with rage.

I could smell blood—it seemed like my sense of smell had suddenly sharpened—and I wasn't sure if it was my blood or my mother's or the wolf's. My head felt light and my knees were weak. I lunged toward the moving truck. My mother slammed the brakes and screamed at me. The silver cross she always wore around her neck glittered harshly in the white winter light.

My body hit the car door and I fell back onto the ground. The impact shook me, woke me up. Scoot was baring his teeth at me through the window.

I was trying to attack my mother. My mother who had taken care of me since I was born. Who had dressed me up like her doll, combed out my waist-length hair and made sure I had the things I needed. She had made photo albums full of pictures of me dressed in the special outfits she got from catalogs or on trips to the city. She was always telling people how pretty and smart and athletic I was, how well I did in school, how if I learned to control my temper I could have everything I wanted when I grew up.

But now I was acting like a monster.

I backed away as she opened the truck door.

"Liv? What the . . ."

I turned—it took all my will—and I ran from her then. I ran and ran until I reached my woods, the woods nearby that I had always loved more than my own floral-print bedroom in my own dollhouse-perfect home. I threw my body in among the trees where everything was dark and so much safer. I didn't understand what happened to me next; I only remember it in fragments, like a dream. My heart pounded in my ears and branches crackled and broke around me. Suddenly I was hot, so hot, I didn't want my clothes. I pulled off my shirt as I ran. My bare shoulders were lashed, bloodied by winter branches like dark arms bearing knives. I fell to the icy ground, to all fours, panting. I tossed my head. My neck hurt, my jaw ached. My eyes burned. The sounds in my ears were furious and loud. I could smell the world. It smelled of fear and sickness and hate. Even the forest smelled like death. My hips felt as if they were being torn apart. I crouched down and then I sprang and then I ran and ran trying to get away from myself and my desire to turn back. And find my pretty, cheerful, slender little mother. And kill her.

Why was I so angry? I asked myself later. My mother had killed a wolf, that's all.

I love animals but that isn't reason enough to feel such rage. My mother is a hunter, like a lot of people in this town; it's what people do here. Animals are more important to me than most humans because they don't judge you and only want your kindness. Now I volunteer one day a week at the pound, cleaning the cages, feeding the dogs. I'd work there more often but I can hardly handle one day; it breaks my heart to see the dogs and I always want to bring them home but my mom says no dogs except for Scoot.

My mother says she loves animals, too. She says there is nothing more beautiful than the thrill of shooting a deer as it runs through the brush. She says a great hunter almost becomes one with her prey.

I wish I didn't feel so much anger toward my mother but I can't help it. I feel less like my mother's daughter every day of my life since practically the moment I turned thirteen. After that I began to question if she was really my mother at all. And then I began to question myself. Because what kind of daughter feels that way? What kind of freak beast— But I can't think like that. If I do I will get too angry at myself. I can't let myself get angry at all. Anger changed me once in a terrible way I do not understand. Who knows what else I could do.

After what happened on my thirteenth birthday, they took me to a psychiatrist named Nieberding who had the head of an elk mounted on his wall. He was a tall, thin, balding man with a fringe of hair around his ears. He shook my hand and then fell back onto his reclining chair. It made a loud sound as it adjusted to his weight. Nieberding scowled almost petulantly at my hands—maybe he was noticing that my middle fingers are disproportionately long—as he leaned back in his big chair, his legs stretched out in front of him and his fingertips pressed together like pursed lips.

"So, Olivia, do you know why you are here?" he asked me.

"Liv," I said.

"Liv. All right. Do you know why you're here?" He paused. "Liv?"

"My mother sent me."

"There was an incident, she said."

I shrugged.

The doctor made a note on his pad. He continued to ask me questions about my parents, my friends, school. I evaded everything. Finally he asked again,

"What happened the other day, Liv?"

"I don't know," I said. "Sorry." I really was, too. I wanted to tell him something so he would stop asking questions but my mind was a muddle.

"Your mother tells me you were very upset. After she came back with the wolf in the truck you ran off. Do you remember?"

I shook my head.

"You don't remember anything?" He scowled at me and scratched his chin.

"No," I said. "I just felt really weird. And so I started running. To the woods. I don't know what happened after that." I was afraid to know but I also wished there was someone who could explain it to me. One thing I was sure about—it wasn't going to be Nieberding.

After that session Dr. Nieberding put me on Lexapro and told my mom to get me a journal to write my feelings in. The meds and the diary worked. I rarely got angry anymore. I rarely cried. I was usually quiet and well behaved. I stopped having to see Nieberding except for general checkups to monitor my medication or if I slipped and had a really bad tantrum at school or with my parents.

Most of the time, except maybe for the small, low-set, slightly pointed ears that I hide behind my hair, my very red lips and long middle fingers, I pass as normal. I can seem like any other relatively healthy seventeen-year-old who goes to school and work, loves animals, loves the woods, loves her boyfriend and never thinks about how lucky she is to have functioning body parts, like eyes or hands.

But, really, I am different from any seventeen-year-old I know because of the thing that happened to me when I was thirteen years old. Whatever it was.

Corey

The woods at the edge of the town where we live are thick and dark, and my boyfriend, Corey, and I go there together even though we aren't supposed to. There have been four murders in those woods—still unsolved by my dad, the chief of police, and his men—and most people don't go there without a gun, although guns didn't stop the murders on those full moon nights four years in a row. But the victims of the full moon murders were all hunters, and Corey and I love the woods too much to stay away.

As a little girl I would always go to those woods

alone. I did it because I was much less afraid there than I was everywhere else. Not that it was obvious why I would have been afraid in my parents' nice house with the flowery rugs and satin pillows and the pretty garden. It seemed like a good life from the outside. But I'd always felt that somehow I was too different to ever really fit in that world. The woods were where I belonged. My parents said it was dangerous there, that I shouldn't go by myself, even though the murders hadn't occurred yet. My mom and dad didn't know that I snuck away every chance I got.

My footsteps were silent on the mulchy ground. The white bark of the aspen was rough, and the yellow, almost heart-shaped leaves were soft. Each tree seemed to have a soul, something deep inside it, just like humans did. I wondered if trees yearned, loved, grieved. I had a favorite oak with a large hollow that I could fit inside. I would tuck my feet under me and sometimes I even slept there.

Once I found a log cabin there in the woods. It was

built among the trees so it looked like not a single tree had been felled to accommodate it and because of this it had an odd, rambling shape. You almost couldn't see the cabin for all the trees that grew around it. There was a trail of smoke coming from the chimney and nine pairs of boots—two large and seven smaller ones—were by the door. There was a well and a small vegetable patch and a chicken coop filled with shrieking, fluttering birds.

I wanted to knock on the door so badly; I was so drawn to that cabin, as if it contained something or someone I needed. I held my breath for a second, felt my heart rate quicken as I started toward the door. But, no, I couldn't go there. It wasn't for me. Not yet.

When I went back to look for it again I could never find it. It was as if someone had put some kind of glamour, some kind of spell, on that ground, and I felt as if I was walking in circles around it again and again, never able to see what was in front of my eyes.

That was also how I felt about what had happened

to me when I was thirteen. I felt as if I was always cir-
cling around in my own brain trying to understand.

I've never been able to figure it out and I've never
seen the cabin again but Corey and I imagine this is
our real home, a house made of roots. I feel better here
than in my little-girl room with the stuffed animals
and the canopy bed. It's hard to breathe there. Everything smells of sickly sweet air freshener, bleach and
toxic cleansers. In the woods it smells bittersweet, of
leaves and earth. The air is humid and sticks to us like
clothes. The fireflies glow—our lanterns, keeping us
safe. We find a moss bed among the roots of a tree and
we are quiet. I hardly need to say any words to Corey.
We understand each other without words. I can tell
just by looking at him if he is happy or sad, if he isn't
feeling well and if he wants to make love, which is
pretty much always, but we don't. Dried leaves crunch
beneath our small bodies as we roughhouse on the
damp, mossy ground. The light is dappled and dark
green. My hands reach up and stroke Corey's face. His

cheeks are smooth—he still doesn't need to shave—
and his nose is broad. He puts his soft, full mouth
over mine and I feel the fatigue leaving me. Here we
escape our families but also time and even our bodies.
We become something else altogether.

My parents don't know about Corey. They would
never admit it but the color of his skin makes a dif-
ference to them. I have to hide our relationship from
them and every day it gets harder.

Corey Steele and I met when we were in first grade.
For a long time we thought of each other as just being
there, sort of permanent fixtures in the classrooms as
we passed through elementary school. We were always
in the same class but we never really talked. Still, I
always looked for him on the first day and I always
made sure I knew where he was on the playground,
who he was playing with, what he was wearing. He
told me he had the same feelings about me. He remembered things I said and did as a kid in perfect detail.

Most people thought I was weird but Corey seemed to admire me. Like how I got in trouble for screaming at Kenny Martin because he called Sadie Nelson, the girl who didn't come to my birthday party, fat. (When I reminded Sadie of this after she didn't show up to my party, she told me she hadn't needed me to defend her; it just made her look worse and more unpopular.)

Corey was the quiet, kind one. He told me he usually just felt invisible. He was one of a very few black kids in the school and I was always on the alert, waiting to pounce on anyone who made a racial comment. They never did, at least around me. Maybe they could see in my eyes what I would have done to them.

But sometimes people called Corey other names, maybe because he was so quiet and shy. He hardly said a word and had even been tested for autism because of it. When my mom's bridge club partner's son Dale Tamblin called Corey a retard I scratched him until he bled. I was suspended for a week but Dale Tamblin never bothered Corey again.

Corey and I finally got to know each other better toward the very end of seventh grade. The middle school was a lot bigger and after the first year we started hanging together at lunch because we didn't really know anyone else we wanted to spend time with and it felt like we needed the protection. Neither of us had any close friends. Corey hung out with his brothers on the weekends and I was almost always alone up until we became close. My one friend, Pace, had transferred to a private school where he wore a uniform, continued to excel at sports and pined after boys in secret and on the phone to me.

One spring night before I became really close to Corey, I snuck out of the house and rode my bike to a party on the outskirts of town. It was in a big farmhouse and a metal band was playing in the barn. I only liked alternative music and the screeching guitar was giving me a headache. There were a lot of older kids there, but a few of the cool kids from my class, too; I'd overheard them talking about the party—that's how I knew about it. I'm not sure why I went: I guess I was just restless. Everything had been different after the incident with my mother and the wolf. I was always jittery when the sun went down. My skin itched. I lay awake smelling the night, wanting to be out in it.

That night I had called Corey but he didn't answer so I went to the party alone. I had some beer from the keg and I was standing by myself, almost hypnotized, staring into the bonfire when Carl Olaf came over to me. He looked pretty cute and his dimples popped out when he grinned.

"Hey. Liv, right?"

I nodded and smiled but tried not to let my teeth show. They are small and sharp; I thought they looked weird. I kept staring into the fire. My cheeks flamed with heat.

"You've got pretty hair."

I thanked him.

"Can I get you another PBR?"

I held out my plastic cup and he went to refill it.

When he came back he took my hand and we sat in a dark corner of the barn. The animal smell made my head spin.

"You don't have too many friends, huh?"

I shook my head.

"And you don't say a lot."

I shrugged. I could get like this with people, almost mute in spite of the outbursts I had from time to time. I noticed that it happened to Corey, too—the muteness. But later, when we got closer, it didn't happen to us with each other.

I wanted Carl Olaf to kiss me, then. I wanted it because I didn't want to be the weird girl without any friends. I was sick of being weird. My mother had never been weird. Beauty queens were not weird. Bridge club presidents were not weird.

Carl Olaf pulled me behind the chicken coop. He told me that my lips were the reddest he had ever seen. I do have very bright red lips—it embarrasses me. "You're not wearing lipstick, are you?"

I shook my head no.

He pulled me down into the straw and kissed me and I let him. I didn't mind. I kissed him back.

Then Carl Olaf put his hand up the back of my shirt. He hesitated. His fingers made their way around to the front. He let them linger over my breast. He pulled my bra to the side and stroked. He gasped. He pulled his hand away.

"What the fuck," he said.

I jumped to my feet with my hands across my chest.

"It's true," he said. "It's true." He was laughing. "I Iairy teets!" He got up and staggered away, sniggering.

I had a thin layer of downy, reddish hair on a lot of my body that had started growing when I turned thirteen. When I saw it I thought I looked beastly; no boy would ever love me. My mom took me for painful laser treatments to remove it but they hurt so much. Waxing and shaving didn't last. Sherry Lee and Kelly Reddy must have told Carl. They were girls without even a trace of stubble on their smooth, tan bodies and they had roared with laughter when they saw me change my clothes in PE. Once they tied my hair to the back of my chair during math class.

I suppose I am lucky that I didn't have my period that night, that it was one night short of a full moon, that I was on Lexapro to quiet my anger, so that I didn't try to attack Carl Olaf the way I had tried to attack my mother.

But Carl Olaf was really the lucky one. At least that night.

Something had risen up in me when he laughed. The animal smell of the barn grew overwhelmingly strong and seemed to have seeped inside of me. The heat of the bonfire where we had stood before now seemed to burn on my skin. I wanted to scream with rage and lash out at Carl with my nails and teeth. I knew these feelings had to do with what happened on my birthday the winter before, but I didn't understand them. What I did know was this: This thing, whatever it was—it was inside of me and I knew I had to keep it there.

Carl Olaf was lucky that night but not the next. The following night Carl's father, Reed Olaf, was the first known victim of the full moon murderer, killed in the woods while he was out hunting deer. My father and his men never caught the killer. I felt terrible for Carl but I never got to give him my condolences because he always leered at me and called me names before I had the chance.

As I was leaving the party on my bike, that night before Carl's father died, before I had any sympathy for him at all, I saw by moonlight seven boys coming up the dirt road that ran through the cornfields from the town. The boys all had sleek features, dark hair and gold-colored eyes. One of them walked ahead of the others. He was the tallest and he had a fierce expression on his face. The best-looking boy I had ever seen.

Something was wrong, I could tell; the boys seemed

angry about something, or just very determined, in the way they walked so precisely, two rows of three behind the tall boy, shoulder to shoulder, trudging along the road. I was afraid of them but also drawn to them. I hurried past, trying to keep my head down, but I wanted to stare. When I passed by, I looked back. My face was burning with blood as if I were still gazing into the bonfire. The tallest, most beautiful boy had stopped in his tracks and fixed me with his golden gaze. I could feel him reaching inside me, illuminating the dark, hidden tissue of my brain with the flashlight of his mind. It hurt and felt pleasurable at the same time and I gasped.

What happened? he asked me, without words.

How could he do that? I wondered. How could I hear him? But just in case he could hear me, too, I thought back at him as hard as I could: *I was shamed.*

He nodded as if he understood.

Who was this strange boy and why was he here with the six other boys and why did he notice me? But I didn't want to know the answers to these questions, not really. Somehow I knew that I shouldn't go there, that it was dangerous. So I tried to forget about him.

I rode my bike as fast as I could all the way home.

When I got there I called Corey but I never told him what happened at the party. I was afraid he wouldn't like me if he knew so I wrote about it in my diary later that night and left it at that. But just hearing Corey's voice made me feel better, soothed.

We hadn't kissed or anything yet at that point. We just hung out in the woods and talked. Or sometimes we were just quiet for hours.

We listened to music, too. Corey was always finding the perfect music for me, for us. I asked him to try to find something that would make me cry because I was sick of how numb the meds left me and even though I loved the carefully mixed CDs with names like Tears for Liv, they never quite worked. He brought me every version of Sia's "Breathe Me" and that finally did the trick one night, even with the antidepressants.

I didn't even know how in love with Corey I was. It was more the way you feel about your eyes, or your hands. You just can't imagine it being any different.

We kissed finally when we were fourteen. I hadn't really wanted to before, not after the thing with Carl Olaf and also that other thing. Meaning the thing with my mom and the wolf—whatever it was—that I didn't like to think or talk about. I was afraid that what happened to me after I saw the dead wolf in the truck could happen again if . . . I didn't know if what. . . . If I got angry, of course, but also maybe if I got too excited, or let myself go out of control. But at a certain point Corey and I couldn't resist and we just kissed and nothing bad happened. It was so sweet and magical and natural, and I didn't change in any bad way. I just started liking myself a little more and having more confidence. I guess I just felt more complete.

26

Now, three years later, I touch Corey's short brush of dark hair. I can almost feel it buzzing with growth under my fingers. I run my hands over his slender forearm, the well-formed slope of bicep with its delicate tracing of veins. His skin is smooth and very dark. I try to understand, but I don't. I can't understand why it would matter. Corey could have scales or fur and I would love him, but this is skin, beautiful skin. He smells musky and clean. Today he feels healthy, frisky but calm; I can tell. He stares out into the dark forest and then he looks back down at me. The almost-always-tense muscles in my neck and shoulders relax under his gaze. I know he won't judge the length of my fingers, the way soft hair grows on my body. He doesn't seem to mind anything about me at all.

He tells me, "That's love, Liv. When you accept everything about the other person."

I hope that he can accept everything about me, I really do.

✴ ✿ ✴

We were in the woods, just like this, when we saw the gray wolf.

She came and stood watching us from the under-brush, her pale eyes glamorously lined and her muzzle quivering with information.

The wolf population is very small. They are endan-gered, those wolves, and you almost never see them.

Corey grabbed my wrist and we sat motionless watching her before she vanished into the woods again.

"She reminds me of you," he whispered. "Beautiful and wild."

When I looked back at Corey there was awe in his eyes.

The day dissolved into evening around us. We were so mesmerized by the wolf and each other that it seemed we could not move from the spot, until it got very late. Corey kissed my neck and pressed his face against mine. We shivered. The night was coming and we would have to go home.

When I stood up, Corey grabbed at my legs and wrestled me back to the ground. We rolled in the soft mulch and leaves caught in our hair. I pressed my face into his chest and tried to curl up smaller against him so I would never have to leave.

How will we leave this place? How will we return home? When this is the only home.

My mother looked up from the kitchen sink where she was washing the pots and watching *American Idol*. My dad and Gramp were watching the news on the TV in the living room. There was a TV in almost every room of the house and my parents usually left them on when they went out of the room—I was always going around turning them off. All I could see of my father was his ex-quarterback shoulders and the top of his dark hair. My grandfather was a little white head peeking over the top of the overstuffed floral sofa. I could smell corn dogs and coleslaw.

"You missed dinner, hon," my mom said. "Are you

hungry? I'll make you something."

My stomach growled in answer but I shook my head. "I'll just get a sandwich." I opened the refrigerator.

"Wash your hands!" she said.

I took out cheese, bread and mustard and laid them out on the table. I glanced at the cold cuts and shut the refrigerator door. I have to admit I crave meat but I am still a strict vegetarian.

My mother was watching me. "You have leaves in your hair."

I reached up and felt the crunchy leaves, rubbed them until they disintegrated. The smell reminded me of Corey.

"Liv," my mother said, "where do you go? I hope it's not the woods. We worry."

My dad turned off the sound and looked over at us. He was drinking his scotch. "Damn right," he said.

"Hi, Liv," said Gramp. "How's my girl?"

I went over and kissed his cheek. "Good, Gramp.

How are you?" He smiled like a kid and then took the remote and put the TV sound back on.

"You didn't answer the question," my mom said.

"I was at Pace's."

She squirted more soap into the sink. She was wearing a flowered apron and high heels. She said it was good exercise for her calf muscles to wear them as much as possible.

"Maybe you want to invite Pace to Gramp's birthday party," my mom said.

I nodded and poured myself a glass of water. "Yeah, maybe." As I lifted the glass to my lips I smelled my sleeve as surreptitiously as possible for a whiff of Corey's scent still lingering there.

"Liv?" My mother spoke eagerly, like she wanted to connect with me, bring me out of my daze.

I tried not to sound annoyed with her. "Yeah?"

"I found you a cute dress in the Nordstrom catalog. I want you to look nice for the party."

"Okay, thanks." I was trying to be positive but I

knew I wouldn't like the dress she picked. I also knew I'd probably end up wearing it for her anyway. I took my sandwich and headed for my room.

"Liv! What did I tell you about walking on your toes?"

"I always walk on my toes," I mumbled. I'd given up trying not to sound annoyed.

"You'll get shin splints. And put those jeans in the wash; they're filthy." I heard her sigh loudly as I closed my bedroom door behind me.

Pace

In order to hide my relationship with Corey from my parents I pretend to date Pace McIntyre. Pace looks just the way my parents would want my boyfriend to look. He is tall and fair and athletic, a football player, even. A lot of girls crush on him.

I've known Pace since we were ten. Our mothers play bridge together and our fathers coach Little League. The first time I saw him was at a party at our house. He was standing by himself looking uncomfortable and cringing whenever an adult came up to tell him how tall and handsome he was or to brush his hair out of his eyes. We went to my room and he took a cassette tape out of his pocket and played me Tori Amos songs on my boom box.

"You even look like her," he said.

Well, I loved him from then on and he told me he felt the same way about me, even though the only music I had to play him at that time was Britney Spears. But we were friends instantly; even before we knew the truth about each other we sensed that the other had a secret, although at least Pace actually knew what his secret was.

Sometimes Corey, Pace and I hung out, too, but I knew it made Pace feel like the third wheel and it made Corey a little jealous so we usually didn't. They weren't really close—maybe because of how close I was to both of them—but they liked each other. And when I was with them at the same time I felt the best I ever felt—safe like I had my pack.

Pace called me the night Corey and I saw the wolf. I could tell something was up with him. His voice sounded excited and a little out of breath. We talked about the usual—summer jobs and music and things. I was working at the ice cream parlor and Pace was a waiter at a quaint little café, with tiny flowers on the wallpaper and paintings of boats in carved wooden frames, where he served cucumber and cream cheese sandwiches with tea to little old ladies. We both tried to play our own music whenever we could get away with it but usually the managers didn't let us. Both Pace and Corey were always turning me on to new songs and quoting lyrics and trying to decipher what they meant. Which was how I felt talking with Pace that night; he was being so cryptic. "You're like a song by the National," I told him. "All mysterious and shit."

"Okay," he said finally. "I met someone."

I smiled into the receiver. Pace had been looking for a boyfriend for years. The reason he posed as my boyfriend was as much to hide being gay from his parents and the rest of our less-than-tolerant town as it was to keep my parents from finding out about Corey. He calls me Skirt and I call him Beard, although technically he isn't really my beard but, as Corey says, my white beard.

"Dude!" I said. "Scoop, please."

"Well, he's not straight." Pace always crushed on straight guys and it never worked out.

"That's a good start!"

"Hottie," he said.

I laughed. "Naturally. What's his name?"

"Michael. It's so weird. I was walking home and I passed that old house on Green?"

"The Fairborn house?" It was a big, old Gothic place with gargoyles cowering under the eaves and years' worth of old Christmas trees planted in the yard. No one had lived there in forever and it was a wreck, coated in dirt and cobwebs. There was a rumor that the teenage son of the man who built it had hung himself in the dining room. Once I snuck out of my house and met Corey and Pace for a midnight picnic under the fir trees. We took photographs to see if we could find ghosts captured in the shots but nothing turned up except the shadow of the pine needles.

"Yeah. And there was a light inside. So I thought I'd check it out. It was unlocked and there's this guy sitting at a table with a jar full of lightning bugs."

"Crazy!" I said. "Why was he there?"

"He said he just really liked it."

That was like us—like Corey and Pace and me. We loved to explore places that we thought were haunted, like the old steel mill, a campus dorm called Ravenwood Hall and the cracked stone ruins—some partial pillars, steps and foundation—of the orphanage that had once stood at the edge of the forest. The owner was said to have gone crazy and burned it down with a hundred screaming children inside. We never found anything unusual there except that when we left there were tiny handprints on Pace's Jeep.

"Does he go to St. Paul?" I asked Pace.

"No, he said he's homeschooled. He just moved here."

I heard a click and my mom's voice. "Oh, sorry. You're on the phone? Did you get your homework done?"

"I'm talking to Pace, Mom."

"Hi, McIntyre." I hated when she called him by his last name; it sounded too coy and flirtatious when she did, even though a lot of people called him that and I knew she was just trying to be nice.

"Hello, Mrs. Thorne."

"I don't want to disturb your conversation but it's getting late."

"We'll be right off," I said.

She hesitated, then hung up.

"Shit," Pace said. "Why does she always do that?"

I flopped onto my back on my bed and let my hair hang down over the side so that it swept the floor. "I told her I was with you today."

"What else is new?"

"I know. I just forgot to tell you."

"I've always got your back."

"Same here. Tell me more about this guy you met."

"He's just really cool. Not like anyone else. He asked me a lot of questions but he didn't talk about himself at all. There was something really sad about him, though."

"You and I like those melancholy types, huh?"

I knew him well enough to be able to hear the smile on the other end of the line. "How's the boy?"

I lifted my legs in the air and examined my feet. My toes have very slight webbing between them that had seemed to have become more noticeable in the last few years and I never wore open-toed shoes anymore. There were a few hairs sprouting from my big toes. I reached for tweezers.

"Pace," I said. "It was so cool! We saw a wolf today!"

"A wolf?" I imagined Pace in his big room in his big house—an overdecorated Colonial like ours—wearing sweats and a T-shirt, his golden hair falling across his forehead. He let me comb his hair and sometimes

I put mascara on his eyelashes. He's as gorgeous as a model but it just seems to freak him out.

"Yeah. In the woods. A gray wolf. A female, I think. She just stared at us and then ran away."

Pace is the person who knows me best. I want to tell Corey about the strange thing that happened to me when I turned thirteen but I'm afraid. It's not because I don't trust him; I trust him more than anyone. But if he got scared by what I told him and decided to leave me I think I would literally die.

I went to Pace at dawn after the night of my thirteenth birthday and threw pebbles at his window. I stood naked and shivering behind a tree, not sure what had happened or why I was there at all. He came down carrying a blanket, wrapped me up in it, and we sat in his garden and talked while the sun rose bloody above the distant woods.

I told him about my mother and the wolf, how angry I'd felt and how I'd run to the woods but that I couldn't remember much after that. Pace listened and stroked my head and told me I was going to be okay but he didn't try to force me to remember anything that was too scary for me. That was also the night he told me he was gay.

I said it didn't change anything between us. I had kind of known already, anyway. The only thing that worried me about it was that I knew most people in our town wouldn't understand. They rejected me for being weird and hairy, which I understood, but they would also reject handsome, social, athletic, "normal"-seeming Pace for this if they found out. It would be harder for him than for me, I thought. Under his strong exterior Pace was more sensitive than I was. And the cruelest kids might do something worse than just reject him.

But that night Pace seemed relieved to have told me. He gave me a shirt and jeans to wear and walked me home. I snuck into the house and crawled into bed and slept for a day. We never spoke about what had happened to me after that night but we talked about Pace's situation a lot.

"I think that's a good sign," Pace was saying—four years later—about the wolf sighting. "Maybe things are changing for us, Skirt."

In a way I hoped he was right. But there was something about this guy, Michael, about our wolf and even about that word—*change*—that worried me.

Joe

*I*n the morning I rode my bike downtown to the ice cream parlor where I work. My mom and dad know the owner, of course—they know every-body; people jokingly call my mom the mayor—and I figured a summer job there was something to do to keep my parents off my back until I started school at the local college in the fall. It was also a distraction from the fact that Corey and I wouldn't be together then; he was going to school in New York.

It was ninety-three degrees by ten o'clock, with high humidity. Kids were playing in the gray stone fountain already, the way I used to do when I was little. I was jealous of the freedom they had. My mom used to let me run half naked through the water. I remember how she looked at me, then, with the softness in her eyes that hasn't been there for years.

In keeping with the weird Gothic architecture of the town, small severed heads decorated each of the points surrounding the top of the fountain and the water spurted from the mouths of angry-looking water gods. Baskets of purple flowers hung from the old-fashioned streetlamps. The streets around the square were cobbled. It looked quaint and charming unless you knew what was really going on, like most places, I guess. I suppose the fountain gargoyles kind of gave away what was underneath.

I passed some boys from school sitting on a wrought-iron bench.

"Hey, it's hairy teets," one of them said.

It was Carl Olaf.

I'd been hoping that after I'd graduated he would

leave me alone. But I knew that Carl could have associated me with the news of his father's death and with the fact that my father, the police chief, had never found the killer so I'd become more and more withdrawn and on edge around Carl and his friends, always expecting something like this.

"What did you drink to put that hair on your chest, girl?" said another boy. Nick McCain.

"You could use some of it, whatever it is." Carl Olaf shoved him affectionately.

I flipped them off with my long middle finger and rode faster up to the door of the ice cream parlor. It was a relief to be inside, away from them. I served milkshakes and ice cream cones all day in the strawberry pink room with the black-and-white checkerboard floor, the shiny chrome counter. Since the owner wasn't around, I played the Metric song Corey had made for me. "Help, I'm alive."

Corey kept texting me all day from the veterinarian's office where he worked.

when can i c u?

i miss u.

that wolf still in my mind.

liv i love

I got kind of distracted, I guess. At one point a guy came over to me and showed me his dish of melted ice cream. He didn't say anything, just tapped his spoon on the side of his dish.

"May I help you?" I asked.

"This was supposed to be a banana split. Operative word: banana. Do you see a banana?"

"No sir. Did you eat it?"

"You forgot it."

"Sorry, sir." I went to make him another one.

"You Cindy Thorne's kid?"

I nodded.

"You'd never know you're related," he said, and leaned back against the wall with his meaty arms folded on his chest, waiting for his banana split. "And you don't look nothing like your dad either."

I'd heard that, too. A lot. Both my parents have dark hair and blue eyes. My dad is tall and broad and my mom is small and curvy. There isn't a sign of red hair, green eyes or wiry bodies in the whole extended family as far as I know.

After work, I rode home down the cobbled street past a row of small brick buildings with pointed leaded-glass windows. There was an antique store that smelled of mothballs and was filled with carved wooden angels, leather-bound trunks, mismatched china and old lace dresses. There was a shoe repair shop, a dusty book-store, a small market, a drugstore and a beauty salon. I came to Joe Ranger's prosthetics shop.

About twenty years ago this town was all about the steel mill that my grandfather once owned; it now sits abandoned at the outskirts of town—a big brick building with two metal towers. Corey and Pace and I go there sometimes because it's said to be haunted, and you'd believe it by the way it looks and because of how many people died there in blasts of white heat or bone-crushing slams of metal. Once we thought we heard someone screaming.

Joe Ranger's father's prosthetics shop used to do a lot of local business from all the steel mill accidents but things have slowed since the mill closed. The prosthetics have gotten much more high-tech than the ones Joe makes. He works construction to pay the bills. It's a shame he has to use his genius hands that way, if you ask me, but "You gotta do what you gotta do," as Joe says.

In spite of the economy and the shutting of the steel mill, Joe kept the store open part-time. He seemed to like making the limbs and some people sought him out specially because he's what they call a genuine genius craftsman. The limbs hung on the walls of the dim shop; they were so lifelike they disturbed me. There were body parts of all different shapes and sizes, even some tiny ones for children. I tried to imagine what it was like to be missing a body part like that, to have to strap on an arm and a leg, how it must hurt and how strong you had to be, physically to get around and mentally not to want to die. It was hard enough for me being alive with a fear of my own anger.

Joe was standing out in front, smoking a cigarette. His yellow dog, Cooper, was panting in the shade. When Joe saw me he tossed his ciggy to the sidewalk and put it out with the toe of his work boot.

"Hey, darlin'. How's my little digitigrade?"

"Shut up," I said in my sweetest voice. Joe liked to tease me about how I walked on my toes—a digitigrade. I sat down on the ground next to Cooper and took his large, adorable yellow face in my hands, looked into his downward-sloping brown eyes as we put our noses together and he licked me. I knew it was risky relaxing with them like this—my parents had told me not to hang around Joe Ranger—but after seeing Carl Olaf, I needed Joe's company.

Joe hadn't shaved and his reddish whiskers covered his cheeks. He watched me with his fiercely green eyes.

"Everything cool with you?"

I shrugged. "It's okay."

"I'm not convinced," said Joe, scanning my face.

I felt like telling Joe about the boys calling me names but I decided against it. I trusted him but you never knew what Joe Ranger would do to anyone who hurt me. There was something a little off about him.

For some reason he'd taken a liking to me and had always been kind of protective. I liked him, too. He knew a lot about animals. There were always stray dogs coming into his shop, cats, too. I tended to trust people who animals liked that way. Joe was the only adult in town who seemed to just get me, without judging or even asking any questions. But I couldn't spend as much time with him as I'd have liked because of my parents. When I asked why they didn't want me over there, they wouldn't answer. Just mumbled something about bad news. My dad told me I better stay away but I still managed to get in a quick chat every once in a while and I'd never gotten busted.

"Hey, I gotta go," I said, giving Cooper's ears a last scratch.

"You let me know if you need anything," Joe said as I hurried away.

To get to the vet's office where Corey worked I had to ride across the deserted campus of the liberal arts college, with its American Gothic architecture of high-pointed, cross-gabled roofs, towers, pavilions and sharp arches. I'd never liked the style; it gave me the creeps. So did the deserted houses surrounding the campus. About half the town population is students who go away in the summer, leaving the old wooden houses near campus empty and moldering in the wet, hot heat.

By the time I got to Corey's work I was sticky with sweat. He came out wearing his green scrubs and leading three dachshunds. They panted in the humidity and strained at the leash when they saw me but he spoke softly to them and they sat down. Dogs listen to Corey like that. I scratched the head of the littlest one and he poked his nose up at me.

"Who are these guys?"

"Mugs, Snugs and the Weiner."

"Seriously? The Weiner? People are so weird. How would they like to be called 'the Dumb Human'?"

"Or Penis Head," said Corey. We laughed and I playfully pushed his shoulder but it reminded me of Carl shoving his friend Nick and I stopped smiling.

"I'm almost off. I just got to let these guys pee and then they're going home with old Penis Head," Corey said.

He finished up, changed his clothes and came out to me. We headed straight for the woods.

Corey threw his arm around my shoulders and led me into the trees. "You okay?" he asked. "You're way quiet."

I didn't know why I felt so weird. Maybe it was the hairy comment, but I didn't want to tell Corey about that.

"It's so hot," I said. "I've been feeling spaced all day."

Corey buried his face in my hair. As soon as we were under the cover of the trees our bodies just naturally drew together like that. "You smell like sugar," he said.

"I know. It's gross."

"Not as bad as sick cat." Corey sniffed his arm. "Poor Mewriel."

"Mewriel? Will she be okay?"

"Leukemia."

We held a spontaneous moment of silence for Mewriel.

"I want to take a bath," I said softly, wishing I could rinse off sadness and shame that easy.

"Well, come on, girl."

We found the stream, trickling among the trees, shallow water reflecting the evening sun in silver fish slivers. I took off the red-and-white-striped shirt I had to wear to work and my white jeans that were

soiled from sitting on the sidewalk, but I kept my
bra and underwear on. Corey stripped down to his
boxers and waded into the deepest part of the water,
began to splash himself off. I did the same. We lay on
our bellies in the muddy streambed, feeling the gentle
current pass over us. Corey's skin gleamed with a thin
film of bright water. I wondered how much longer we
would be able to wait.

Corey and I had decided not to make love yet. It
was crazy in a way, considering how much we loved
each other, how much we wanted to. But I was afraid
for some reason, and Corey was patient with me. I
didn't understand why I was hesitating. All I knew
was that my fear was connected to the thing about
me that I didn't understand—the thing that had happened four years ago. There was too much mystery
around that time. I wanted to know who I was before
I gave a part of myself away.

At the same time, I wondered if my decision was the
right one. Corey and I were going to be separated in

just a couple of months. Even though we'd made plans to visit each other, I knew it wouldn't be the same. And I worried that if we didn't make love soon it might be even harder for us to stay together after the separation.

I closed my eyes, watching the play of light and shadow through my eyelids as Corey pressed his mouth to mine and kissed me softly.

"It's hard for me to wait," he whispered when we finally broke apart.

"I know," I said. "It's hard for me, too. I'm sorry, Corey."

He rolled off of me and looked away among the trees, looked right toward the place where we'd seen the gray wolf. I held my hand out, wanting to stroke his back, but hesitating so that my fingers lingered in the air a few inches from his skin. What if my touch made it all worse?

"When we met," he said, "I felt like such a freak, like no one got me except for you. I couldn't even talk to people."

"I understand," I said. "I only have you and Pace."

"I'm lucky that I know you, Liv. I tell myself that every day."

"I'm lucky, too." I wanted him to feel better so I grasped for something to say but it wasn't exactly the truth even though I wanted it to be. "You're my twin."

Corey picked up a pebble and tossed it lightly into the brush. "We're very different, baby."

"We're not." I paused. "If I were a boy, I'd be you."

"No, you wouldn't."

He was right in a way; we were different but I didn't want to admit it. I *wanted* us to be the same but we weren't. Corey didn't get angry much. Sometimes I wished he did so that I didn't feel like the only one struggling to control myself all the time.

"Why do you say that?" I asked.

"First of all, you don't understand what it's like to live in this town with this color skin." He said it kindly but it stung anyway.

"I understand about being different," I said softly.

"And it's not just that," said Corey. "I don't know if I'm enough for you."

"What are you talking about?" I finally let my hand rest on his back.

"I feel like such a fucking wimp sometimes."

"Don't say that! Don't be so mean to yourself!"

He shrugged. "It's just the truth. But I'll change someday. I hope you can wait for me."

"I don't want you to change at all," I said, and he smiled back at me but it was a sad smile, only with his mouth and not his eyes, as if he didn't quite believe me.

"And I'm going to wait for you," Corey told me. "As long as it takes. I'm not going anywhere."

The Pack

On Sundays I cleaned the cages at the pound. Every time it was so hard to leave without a dog, but my mom and Scoot wouldn't tolerate any other pets. That Sunday there was a black-and-white beagle mix that was beating her tail so hard against the concrete floor that it had started to bleed. I cleaned her up and bandaged her. She licked my face and stared at me with a miserable cockeyed gaze that made my heart feel like her bleeding tail. There was a huge Great Dane mix that hardly fit in the cage. He was a prince; he shouldn't have been there at all. He should have been roaming the primeval forest beside his royal oak-leaf-crowned owner, like something right out of a fairy tale. There was a tiny terrier with one eye. No one would take him home. He seemed to know it, too. He hardly moved from the floor, his cracked, dry nose pressed down between his paws.

So far I'd been able to handle the work, the sad-eyed dogs, the smell in the cages—the defecation and the sickness and the sorrow. I told myself it was more important to take care of the animals than to let my feelings get in the way. But that Sunday the smell seemed to have gotten inside of me so that it was hard to breathe, and with each breath I thought of all those animals that would be lethally injected because they were taking up too much space on the planet.

When I left the pound I was near tears. Everything over the past few days had been building up, making me more sensitive. I couldn't get the dogs' faces out of my mind. I didn't want to be alone with the image of their mournful eyes; I needed my pack.

I texted Corey and Pace and told them to meet me downtown.

freaking out need my guys

We could get free food at the café where Pace worked so we went there. All the old ladies stared at us from their needlepoint chairs. Pace smiled and said hello and then they contentedly went back to their soup. He had one of those smiles, so white and shiny you forgot everything else. We ordered burgers—mine was a veggie—and iced tea from Carolyn Carter, the pretty blond waitress who had a crush on Pace. She didn't like me at all because she thought we were going out (*Why would he go out with her?* I could feel her thinking), so I tried to be extra nice but it was hard to talk.

"What's wrong, Skirt?" Pace asked.

"I just couldn't take the pound today."

"It's rough, huh?" Corey took a bite of his burger.

"I sometimes think you shouldn't do it."

"It's better than not doing it. Somebody has to."

He put his arm around me and kissed my ear. I moved away slightly, aware of Carolyn. Pace and I still needed to keep our cover.

"Not if it messes with you. It's not worth it," Corey said.

"There was a beautiful Great Dane. Or part. Want him?"

"My mom would kill me. I can't bring any more males into that house." Corey had two brothers.

"I want him," Pace said. He lowered his voice. "I heard cute dogs are real guy magnets."

"Really? You'd take him!" I grabbed Pace's hand across the table. Corey looked at our interlaced fingers.

"Yeah. My mom said we could get a dog. She thinks it would be good for me to have something to take care of."

"I love you!" I squealed. "Can you go tomorrow?"

Pace said sure. He could make decisions like that without asking his parents; they always said yes to him about that type of thing. When they first suspected he was gay they sent him to a therapist who then hospitalized him for a while. He had never quite gotten over the experience. That was one reason he'd agreed to be my pretend boyfriend; it kept him safe, too.

When we left the restaurant I flung my arms around Corey and kissed his cheek. I could tell he felt bad that I had to pretend we weren't together in front of Carolyn. He pouted for a second—it was so brief no one would have caught it except for me—then kissed me back. Pace got what had happened, too.

He said, "Next time maybe we'll go out of town to the drive-in and I'll ask that guy Michael and we'll have us a double date."

I wondered, then, as I had wondered before, if I should tone down my affection for Pace around Corey since I couldn't publicly express my feelings for my boyfriend at all. I hated how we couldn't be who we really were in our town.

But then I forgot about it; everything seemed fine between the three of us.

Bad Business

Before Gramp's ninetieth birthday party my mom wanted me to get my body waxed. I didn't feel like fighting anymore; in spite of how much it hurt, it worked better and lasted a lot longer than shaving and the weather was so hot I'd have to have my legs and arms exposed to all the eyes of my parents' friends. So I went.

The beauty parlor was downtown near Joe Ranger's shop. My mom hurried by there as she always did.

"Why do you always run past there?" I asked as she opened the door of the beauty parlor and shooed me inside. I knew she wouldn't answer, though. She didn't like to talk about why she'd blacklisted Joe.

We were blasted by air-conditioning and the fumes of nail polish and bleach. Melanie's House of Beauty was a tiny place with a row of sinks and hair dryers, a couple of nail spas and a back room where, as Pace said, advanced "in-hairoggation" techniques were applied. There were fake pink flowers in a vase and a case full of candy-colored nail polishes and jewel-studded flip-flop sandals.

"Mom?" I said again.

"I don't like that man. I've told you before. I don't like you talking to him."

"But why?" It was one of the conversations we had repeatedly but we never got anywhere with it.

She ignored me and spoke to the woman behind the glass case. "Mel? Hi, we're early for our noon appointment."

The woman stood up wearily. "Hi, Mrs. Mayor."

My mom grinned; I knew she liked that title.

Melanie gestured for me to join her behind the door of the torture chamber. She was a big woman with a deep voice, a beehive hairdo, muscular arms and long fake nails studded with rhinestones. I could have sworn she was really a man.

I lay down on the table and let Melanie baste me with warm pink wax, then apply the strips and rip the hair from my skin. I flinched with each yank. Tears sprang to my eyes.

"What about your bikini line?" Melanie asked. "It's summer!"

"No, thanks."

"You have that cute boyfriend. He'd probably like to see you looking nice in a bikini."

She was talking about Pace. I tried to smile at her. "It's okay."

"Boys don't like to be reminded that their girl is a mammal," she said as she tore a long strip of wax off my calf, leaving a smattering of red bumps and hot pain.

On the way to the car I watched my mom closely. I wanted to see if her expression changed near Joe Ranger's shop. She headed for the other side of the street when he came out.

"Hi, Liv. Mrs. Thorne."

She stopped in her tracks and turned slowly to look at him. Her eyes were bright and alert for danger.

"Hey, Joey," I said.

"Hot one, isn't it?"

I nodded. My mom still stood, frozen. I remembered, suddenly, this happening before, when I was very little. The same trapped-animal look on my mom's face and Joe just watching her like that, like they knew something I didn't. Then it was me who wanted to leave.

I took my mother's hand and we walked across the cobblestone street to the truck.

"Bye, ladies."

Neither of us answered him.

✿ ✿ ✿

During Gramp's party I wore the yellow sundress my mom had ordered for me. I felt like a complete ass in that dress, let me tell you, even with my waxed arms and legs. My mom and I had argued for days about me wearing it and she had won by sheer force of will.

"I'm just trying to help you look pretty, Liv! It's like you think I'm torturing you."

I slumped in my chair and wouldn't look at her. "No, you hire Melanie to do that."

She leaned forward and spoke more softly. "Okay, it hurts to be beautiful. I know, believe me. But I only want to help, can't you see that?"

I thought about all the important things in my life she wouldn't approve of—Corey, my desire to go away with him, my desire for the woods, my friendship with Joey Ranger. Those were the things I'd have to have strength to fight for if it came to that. I couldn't waste my battles on dresses. So I wore the sundress. But I refused to put on the white sandals she got me; I wore my new Chuck Taylors instead.

My mother had invited almost everyone in town, everyone "important" according to her, that is. Gramp had owned the steel mill until it closed, so many of the townies had been his employees. My mom set out platters of cold cuts and cheeses and pastries. There was even her specialty, the dish she made at every holiday—cold shrimp salad with whipped cream. I wasn't hungry.

My mother ran around making sure everyone had a drink. My father was on what looked like his third or fourth scotch. I stood in a corner with Pace, shaking hands and accepting wet kisses on my cheeks from ladies with too much perfume and drunken men who tried to peek down the front of my dress. I muttered thank-yous and nice-to-see-yous. The smell of these people made me feel claustrophobic, like I wanted to go outside, away from the fumes that clung to their hair and clothes.

Dale Tamblin's mother, Nancy, was there. After her husband, Dan, had been killed while he was out hunting in the woods three years ago, she'd stopped going out much, but I guess my mom had persuaded her to come. She'd never forgotten how I'd scratched her son and she gave me a nasty look. I couldn't really blame her, especially after what had happened to her husband.

"Liv!" my mom called from the kitchen. "Bring Gramp his cocktail."

I got the Bloody Mary and carried it over to my grandfather. He wasn't really supposed to drink but my mom said it was a special occasion. I felt weird giving him alcohol, though. This was his second glass. He sat holding court in a high-backed armchair. Gramp looked great for his age, everyone thought so. You could tell that he'd played football as a kid—his shoulders were still broad for a man his age and his hands were huge and gnarled with arthritis.

"Olivia, is that my drink?" he asked.

"Yes, Gramp. Are you sure you want another one?"

I liked my grandfather. I wanted him to be around for

as long as possible.

He winked at me. "Of course. How often do you turn ninety years old?"

"Good point." I handed it to him hesitantly.

"Thank you, Olivia."

"You're welcome, Gramp."

"Would you like a candy?" He reached into his pocket and took out one of the ancient peppermints he carried around with him. They were left over from when my grandmother died fourteen years ago. He had moved in with us after that. Gram always had glass decanters filled with candy all over their house, my mom said. I guess it reminded him of her. My mom complained about her but Gramp called her his angel.

I took the candy to be polite. They were so stale you couldn't crack them with your teeth. Gramp took a large sip of his drink. I wanted to tell him to slow down; I noticed his hand was shaking.

"I miss Ellie," he said.

He talked about my grandmother a lot, especially

at times likes this when we were doing something he would have wanted her to share.

"I know," I said.

"I didn't deserve her." His face was sad and I wanted to comfort him. My grandfather didn't really know who I was, not in a deep way, but he was always kind and seemed to have some special, protective feeling toward me.

"I'm sure you did."

"No." He scrutinized me. "You take after her, you know."

"That's a nice compliment." He'd given it to me before. I didn't look much like Grandmother Ellie, though, and from what I'd heard, our personalities were different, too. But she was quieter than my mom and loved animals, so we shared those things.

"She was a very caring person. She didn't like me drinking, either."

I smiled at him.

"Got me into lots of trouble."

I winked. "Heard it'll do that."

His eyes looked glazed, suddenly. "And she didn't like the hunting. She warned us not to go out that day. But your mother, now she had different ideas about things. Wasn't like her mama at all."

"What's that, Gramp?" I knelt beside his chair and gently pried the drink from his hand. The group of people that had surrounded him had dispersed. I was relieved; I didn't want them to see him like this.

"She shouldn't have killed it," he said. "Your mother. That was some dangerous business. I shouldn't have taken her up in that helicopter. She got the big daddy. She got the leader. That girl came to me after and warned me all about it. But what could I do then? That's some bad, bad business."

I felt weak and steadied myself against the fluffy flowered couch. I felt an arm around my shoulder. It was Pace.

He pointed out through the glass to the garden that sloped down the hillside, getting wilder as it went until it became a gulley leading to the woods. Among the tall oak trees and the ferns I saw a figure standing. It reminded me of the deer that ate my mother's flowers and broke the flowerpots. Whenever I could I chased the deer away before she could get her gun.

This wasn't a deer, though.

It was Corey.

When I looked at him he didn't run away, just stood there, staring at me with his big green-brown, leaf-colored eyes. I always teased Corey about his eyelashes, saying it looked like he curled them. He hated when I said that. He looked back and forth between me and Pace and I reflexively moved away from the shelter of Pace's broad shoulder. I knew what Corey was thinking—I knew him pretty well. He wasn't jealous of Pace for real; he just was getting sick of being left out of parts of my life. I didn't want Corey to feel bad but I also felt upset that there wasn't anything I could do about it; I couldn't invite him in. My mother would have had a fit.

Corey turned away and I caught my breath and felt my blood warm in my veins.

Maybe it was because of the confusing things Gramp had said, or because of the realization that I couldn't let Corey in, but seeing him out there like that made anger toward my mother well up in me. Suddenly my senses sharpened and I could smell the slices of fresh ham, chicken and salami on the serving trays. My heart pounded in my chest. It was like the moment when I found out that my mom had killed the wolf, the moment I had been running from for all these years. But I wasn't going to let the feeling overtake me; I couldn't. I reached into the pocket of my dress for the enamel pillbox with the Xanax in it.

My grandfather's voice startled me out of the trance. "That's why I gave her that cross there. They don't like silver when they're on the attack." The silver cross my mother always wore?

"Gramp! What are you talking about? Who is 'they'?"

He looked back at me and this time his light blue eyes were clear. He smiled sweetly. He had one of those faces wrinkled more by smiles than worry or anger. That made what he had said even stranger. But maybe it was the alcohol.

"Did you take my drink, Olivia?"

"Yes. I think maybe you had enough?"

"Oh, all right. I'll just have some cookies instead. Would you mind?"

"Of course not." I got him his sugar cookies and myself a glass of water to swallow my pill with. When I came back and looked into the garden, Corey was gone.

"Want to go outside?" Pace asked.

I nodded. Maybe Corey was just hiding in the trees a little farther off.

The heat and humidity hit us like a wall after the air-conditioned house. It felt good, though, purifying and real. I took some deep breaths with my mouth closed, whispering the air through my nose and deep in my throat to calm down. I'd had to learn ways to calm myself when I was scared or angry. After what happened when I was thirteen I sensed that knowing how to do this wasn't just important—it might be lifesaving. I felt my pulse; it had slowed. I smelled wet earth and not flesh. Corey really was gone.

"What was that shit about?" Pace asked me.

"He shouldn't drink. I don't know why she lets him drink."

"It is his ninetieth birthday. What's the point in not?"

I ran my hand along the bark of the tree where we'd seen Corey. I pressed my face against the trunk, imagining it was him.

"Dude," Pace said. "What was he talking about, though? It freaked me out."

"He used to take my mom hunting from a helicopter in Alaska when they went on vacation there. She killed this big wolf. She likes to talk about it but he never has before."

Gramp would take my mother out in a helicopter in the winter when the animals were easier to spot, running across the snow, and she would shoot them from the sky. I wonder what it must have been like for them, running free and suddenly this whiz of killing pain from above just grounds them. Usually the animals don't die right away. They get hit again and again. Blood stains the snow. Sometimes I imagine what would happen if my mother didn't have a gun or a helicopter. If she was just on the ground with her fingernails and her bicuspids facing a huge, snarling wolf. She'd never survive.

Pace shuddered. "It was weird. Can't we leave yet? You need to go after your boyfriend and I want to see if I can find Michael."

His eyes twinkled when he said the name and I remembered how excited he'd been about the guy he'd met but I hadn't heard much about it since. "Michael, huh? What's up with that?" I socked his arm.

"What?" Pace batted his eyelashes in an uncharacteristically girly way. "He's cute, that's all." I knew Pace; I could tell there was more to it than that but I let it go.

"*You're* cute." I kissed his cheek. He smelled like soap.

"So are you. Let's get out of here. It makes us less cute."

"I can't," I told him. "I promised I'd stay to the end of this thing." Then I added, "Corey looked pissed."

"No," Pace said. "He's just sad. He misses you."

"Maybe you and I should cool it a little when he's around. He's gotten more sensitive about it."

"Sure. I'm going to go see if Michael is there. Is that okay? Will you be all right without me, Skirt?"

"Yeah, you go, Beard," I told him, breaking off a piece of bark in my hands and holding it up against my cheek. The rough texture of tree skin comforted me.

I could hear my grandfather's voice in my mind. *Bad, bad business.*

Haunted

*P*ace left and the party wound down by evening so I helped my mother clean up and then I texted Corey but he didn't answer so I went to find him.

I went toward the campus, where the streets were quiet, everyone inside hiding from the heat or gone for the summer. The large wood-frame houses with their slightly dilapidated porches and hand-lettered Greek signs all looked deserted. It was true that some of the townies and almost all of the college kids from the frat and sorority houses took off for cooler places in the summer but this much quiet was uncanny. The sun was still as bright as day although it was past six o'clock. I rode my bike down the middle of the street, daring a car to come around the corner, but none did. Then I cut through the campus, along paths that ran among brick buildings and leafy trees, to the other side.

Corey lived in one of the bigger old farmhouses at the edge of town. There were bicycles in the yard and a small, neat vegetable garden with rows of carrots and corn and pea vines clambering up a low metal fence. Corey's brothers, Mitch and Jordy, were playing basketball against the tool shed. They glanced up at me blankly. I smiled at them like usual but they didn't smile back. I always wondered if it was a racial thing or if they just thought I was weird like most people did.

"Corey around?" I asked.

They both shrugged. They were much bigger and lighter-skinned than Corey. He had told me that they didn't dislike me the way I thought; they just didn't care.

I parked my bike and went up to the door. Corey's mother answered, wearing her nurse's uniform. She looked at me suspiciously. "It's not a skin color thing," Corey had reassured me, but you never know; my parents wouldn't have put it that way either.

"He's out," she said. Her face was cold. I wanted her to like me so much. Corey had her hazel eyes.

"Would you tell him I stopped by?"

She hummed a yes as I hurried away.

"Oh, and Olivia?" I stopped and looked at her. "You two be careful running around like you do."

I nodded, glad she had spoken to me but not sure what her tone meant. Was she being protective, or warning me to keep my distance from her son? I couldn't tell.

I went to the woods, to our special place, but Corey wasn't there either. I wished I'd run outside to him right away when I saw him in the garden. I looked around at the dark, towering trees and started to feel a panicky sensation in my chest. Then I had to talk myself down. We'd always been safe in the woods before, right?

I didn't want to let myself think about murders that had occurred annually in those woods over the last four years. One of them was Sadie Nelson's dad, Loudon. After it happened she and her mother moved away and no one heard from them again. There was one more besides Loudon Nelson; Carl Olaf's dad, Reed; and Dale Tamblin's dad, Dan—Bob Lee, the father of Sherry, the girl who had tied my hair to the chair in seventh grade. The bodies of the hunters were so torn up it looked like a wild animal had done it but the precision of the killings—always in the woods, always local hunters of about the same age—made my dad and his men think it was human. They hadn't solved the crimes, though. Maybe that's what Corey's mom was referring to but she'd never said anything like it before. Maybe she was finally seeing how serious things were between me and her son.

I trailed my fingers into the cool water of the stream

and listened to the forest sounds. The branches were crackling and I held my breath. Maybe it was Corey? A feeling of anticipation crawled along my spine like when Corey and I had seen the gray wolf. I turned my head.

There was a woman standing in the shadows of the quaking aspen.

She had gray hair that fell over her shoulders but her face looked young. She wore a gray cotton T-shirt and blue jeans and her eyes were pale blue.

We stayed poised, unmoving, looking at each other until I shifted my weight slightly and then she backed away and disappeared.

I had no idea who the woman was but I knew that seeing her meant something. There was a dreamlike quality about it, like where you know the image you are seeing is a symbol for something very important, a secret that your unconscious wants to reveal to you but can't. I shivered in the heat, the forest suddenly growing cold and full of whispers.

I ran back through the trees into the fading light at the edge of the wood, got my bike and headed home. On the way, I rode past the haunted house. I never lingered there long when I was alone; it gave me the creeps and I only liked to get the creeps when I was with my friends. Was Pace there? I needed to talk to him. Behind the old Christmas trees the gray house loomed up with its high-pitched, cantilevered roof shading the stone gargoyles from the sun. The posts and balconies were carved so elaborately that they looked like lace. Some of the windows were carved into large rosettes. I dropped my bike on the sidewalk and made my way among the fir trees and pieces of broken statuary—I recognized one of the gargoyles, smashed to bits, his leering face more angry than ever in its ruined state—to the porch. The sky was finally getting dark and I could hear the cicadas starting up. Through the pointed arch of the front window I saw a very faint light.

I wondered if Pace was there. I would have just

walked in, but maybe he was with Michael? So I knocked.

"Pace?" I said. "It's me."

I heard sounds inside and then after a couple of minutes the peephole opened, then the huge, heavy door. Pace stood there. His eyes looked very big. They darted around and he wasn't smiling.

"Oh, man," I said. "Do not disturb, huh?"

He glanced back behind him into the darkened house. His voice sounded distracted. "No, it's okay. Come in."

He beckoned for me to follow him into the dusty foyer with the parquet floor and through a door to an old-fashioned parlor with shabby lace curtains and furniture covered with sheets and tarps. A few rays of light came in through cracks in the walls.

"I'm sorry to bug you," I said. "I can't find Corey."

Pace was looking around, not really listening.

"Pace?"

"Oh. Sorry. Where's Corey?"

"I don't know. I tried to reach him. I went to his house. He wasn't there. And then I saw this woman. . . ."

Pace was still looking around, confused.

"Is the guy . . . Michael? I want to meet him."

"Michael?" Pace said softly. His eyes had a soft, cloudy look in the faint light. "He was just here."

"I hope I didn't . . ."

Pace shook his head. "It's okay," he said again. "I don't know where he is. Maybe he went to the bathroom."

"I'm going to go," I told him. "I'll leave you guys alone. I'm going to try Corey again."

I walked back to the front door. The air in the house felt frosty in spite of the heat outside. I wouldn't have been surprised if I could have seen my breath. The quiet made my head hurt.

"Cool place," I said. "I mean, literally, too. It's a little freaky, right?"

"Yeah." Pace looked around with that same vague expression.

"You okay?"

He nodded.

"Call me later." I opened the door and ran down the front steps.

I rode my bike around as fast as I could until my legs were shaking. I wanted to make sure all the upset of the day was wrung out of me before I came home. Maybe it was good that I hadn't been able to find Corey. . . .

Late that night I was lying in bed when I heard a clicking sound against the window. I'd texted Corey about ten times before I'd finally given up and curled into a ball under a sheet.

I looked outside and saw him standing there looking up at me, holding a handful of pebbles. I pulled on jeans and shoes and ran out to him.

"Where were you?" I almost started crying as I

fell against his warm chest. He had the woodsy-clean smell. When he tried to move away I put his arms back around me and clung to him.

"You didn't write me back. Were you mad?" I asked. But he didn't seem mad now.

I felt him sigh almost imperceptibly, not really a sound, just a slight movement of his chest.

"I'm sorry, Liv. I needed some time."

"It's okay." I closed my eyes and hugged him even tighter.

"I know I shouldn't have come by the party but when I saw you with McIntyre, pretending . . . it just makes me sick sometimes. Why we all have to pretend like this."

"I know." I tried to kiss his neck but he moved away.

"Serious, Liv. It's messed up. We should be able to be who we are."

"But I'm not sure I know who I am," I said. "What if who we are isn't okay?"

I wanted to tell him so badly then about what had happened to me when I was thirteen. But I couldn't do it. I was afraid he would leave me if he knew about the rage inside of me and what it had made me want to do. And I was afraid that if we made love, if we got that close, whatever lurked inside me might come out and hurt him somehow, or scare him away. That was the truth. That was why I was waiting. Maybe he sensed it, too, because he didn't push me.

"Who you are is more than okay. I love who you are. What are you so scared of?"

"Everything," I said. "Even you. Especially you. Because you might leave." I buried my face in his neck. "I was so scared today when I couldn't reach you." I didn't tell Corey how scared I was of myself.

"I'm not leaving, baby. I told you I'm never leaving you. I just needed time to cool down. When you looked at me through the window, there was something weird about it. . . ."

I thought of how Corey looked like a deer in my

mother's garden. Gramp had scared me, I was angry and afraid, and then I had wanted to run outside and . . . and what? Grab Corey by the throat, drag him inside?

I was mad, I told myself. Not at Corey. At Gramp for scaring me. At Mom for what she had done to that wolf and whatever it meant now. But in the moment it had all gotten confusing and I hardly knew what I felt.

I didn't tell him that what I was most scared of, most haunted by, was something I didn't understand and could never run away from.

It was myself.

Abstinence

I was sitting at dinner with my parents and Gramp, thinking about the woman I'd seen in the woods. I hadn't had the chance to talk to Corey or Pace about her yet—there had been too many other things going on. But I wanted to find out who she was and there was only one person I could ask. I'd go see Joe Ranger the next day, I told myself.

My dad and Gramp were watching ESPN while they chewed their chicken and Scoot begged for scraps.

My mom was singing softly to herself and flipping

through a gossip magazine. I stacked peas on my fork.

"That Jennifer Aniston really better just face the fact that kids might not be in the picture," my mom said. "She looks good, but still . . ."

I ignored her.

"I mean seriously cuckolded. Angelina Jolie. Can you imagine?"

I stared out the window into the garden looking for deer. Once my mom tripped in her high heels when she was running to get her gun to shoot one. She twisted her ankle and had to stay off it for a few weeks.

"Damn deer," she'd said. "Eating all my flowers and now they're trying to break my leg, too."

"Here're pictures of Angie when she was younger," she said now. "Do you know she had her lips done? And her nose? But the thing is, her lips were actually bigger! It's just ridiculously unfair."

My dad turned up the sound on the TV.

"Jeff," my mom said. "I can't hear myself think."

He shrugged and lowered the sound again.

"May I be excused?" I asked.

"You didn't eat your chicken," said my mom.

"I'm a vegetarian, Mom, remember? I have been for four years."

"But you can eat chicken, right?" She winked at me.

We had this conversation at least once a month. I knew she wasn't stupid; she was just hoping I'd change my mind.

"No. Chicken is animal flesh. I don't eat animal flesh."

"You don't want to become anemic. The Micheners' girl Kim, the oldest one? She's anemic. She only eats pasta. Now she has to take iron pills and you know what they can do to your bathroom habits."

My stomach churned the pasta and peas. I got up.

"Gross, Mom. I have to go."

She watched me walk away. "I'm just trying to get the point across," she said.

***

Later, she came into my room without knocking and sat on my bed. I was reading a Swedish vampire book I'd ordered from Amazon.

"What are you reading?"

I closed the book. I was at the part where the zombie tries to rape the transgendered vampire child but the vampire gets away. "Nothing. Can you try knocking?"

"Sorry. I got lonely out there with your dad. I wanted my little girl's company."

She reached out and patted my leg and I pulled it away. I didn't like her touching me that much anymore. I was afraid she'd start talking about depilatories. I folded my legs under me so she couldn't reach up inside my jeans and feel the hair that had started to grow back. I hadn't shaved yet; it was hard to keep up.

"You know, that Pace is a nice-looking fellow." I wondered if my hairy legs had made her think of him—God forbid my boyfriend would have to touch them.

I nodded, just relieved she still hadn't found out about Corey.

"You know, I remember what it was like when I was young."

Here it comes, I thought.

"But it's really important to abstain. There really isn't another option, except getting married and I know you're not ready for that."

I turned my head away from her and stared at the wall. I had hung a poster of a male and female gray wolf kissing, surrounded by their fuzzy, fat pups. Their gray fur and blue eyes ringed in black reminded me of the woman in the woods.

"What about you and Dad?" I asked. They'd gotten married right after college.

"We were young and we made a mistake," she said.

I looked back at her and she smiled. "Not that you are a mistake. We just might have done things differently."

Yeah, right. Sometimes it felt like my whole life

was a mistake. But I hadn't known that my mom felt her marriage was a mistake from the beginning. I wondered if she would have married my dad at all if she wasn't pregnant; it wasn't okay in her family to be a single mother. My parents didn't seem to love each other anymore. Had they ever?

The thing was, as much as the whole conversation irritated me, I agreed with her about the abstinence; I knew that I wasn't going to have sex yet. But it wasn't for the reason she thought. And the boy she was imagining was the wrong one.

Sasha

fter work the next day I went to see Joe. Cooper was sleeping in the shade out front. I knelt
down and let him lick my face.

"Hey, boy. Where's Joey? Where's Dad, huh?" His
eyes shone beams into me. Dogs saw everything but if
they loved you it didn't matter.

The shop was hot, only a small fan revolving feebly.
The prosthetic limbs hung from the walls. So lifelike:
Joe was an artist. They gave me the creeps. One black
and two ginger cats were sleeping around the fan. Joe
was in the back. He came out to see me and grinned

so all his teeth showed.

"What up, dearest?"

"Hey, Joey."

"Did you bring me some rocky road?"

"I would've but it would melt in five seconds."

"Hot out, huh?" He sat on a stool and wiped his forehead with a rag. "Air's broke and I couldn't get the part to fix it." He took two bottled waters out of a refrigerator and handed one to me. "Take a load off and tell me what's on your mind."

I slumped onto a chair with the water. Joe could always tell when something was up with me. When I was thirteen and the first thing happened, I came to him the next day. I didn't tell him about it. I just sat with him and he rambled on about his childhood, how he used to play in the woods, make sculptures out of clay from the riverbed, how his dad lost a hand to the steel mills and that got him into the prosthetics business, how he used to drink too much until he quit. Because of his serious, gentle tone, it was like he was talking to me about what had happened to me but using different words so I wouldn't get scared and run away.

"Do you know anyone new to town? A woman with gray hair and blue eyes?" I asked.

I wanted to find her. Had I really seen her? It seemed like a dream now, a hallucination caused by the heat and my upset state after not being able to reach Corey.

Joe knew everyone and everyone knew him. He ran the local AA meeting and the whole town came to him with their problems. Well, not everyone. The riffraff, as Joe would say. The rich folk went to my mom and dad for help.

He scowled at me and patted his chest pocket for his cigarettes. "Why you wanna know, Livvy?"

"I saw this woman. In the woods. She was just watching me."

"It freak you out, darling?"

"A little."

"But you want to know more?"

I nodded. "She seemed like she wanted to tell me something."

Joe leaned forward, elbow on the knee of his grease-stained jeans, and tapped his lip with his forefinger. "I guess she wanted you to see her or she wouldn't have let you," he said as if he were talking to himself. Then he added, "That's Sasha, Liv. She's not new to town, just keeps to herself. She and her boys live in a cabin out there in the woods."

"A cabin?" I sat up. "The wood cabin with the well?"

"So you've seen it, huh?"

"Once, years ago. I've been looking for it ever since. I thought I made it up."

"Like I said, she wouldn't have let you see her unless she thought you were ready."

My head started to hurt. What was he talking about? "Joey," I asked. "What's going on?"

"I think it's time for us to go talk to Sasha," Joe said. "You got plans?"

"I'm supposed to meet Corey."

Joe stood up and stretched his long arms above his head. "Up to you," he said. "I close shop in a few."

Joe and I walked for a long time among the dense growth of trees. Sunlight trickled through the greenery and sweat trickled down my neck. Birds, butterflies and squirrels seemed to linger near, drawn to Joe Ranger in some uncanny way. One bird, so blue it looked purple and with a fierce expression, even landed on his shoulder when he stopped really still and called it. When it flew away he continued on, walking ahead, his long legs taking big strides while I scurried to keep up. He didn't look back at me much but he held the branches so that I could pass through unscratched most of the time. Under my feet the earth throbbed with life and I could smell the sap in the trees and the minerals in the mud.

I knew that forest really well but I felt confused, as if we'd been walking in circles. Then Joe stopped suddenly and I almost bumped into him.

There was the cabin.

It looked abandoned except for the chickens squawking in the pen. There were no boots in front and the windows were shut tight. The trees had grown closer around it since the last time I'd seen it; they overhung the tin roof as if trying to protect it.

Joe walked up to the door and knocked gently. He was so tall that he had to stoop down so his head wouldn't hit the porch.

We waited. After a while Joe said, "Looks like they're not home. Maybe I was wrong. . . ."

He came back to where I was waiting. I hadn't wanted to get too close. I turned and started away. I wasn't so sure about this idea after all, anyway.

Just then we heard a sound and the cabin door opened. The gray-haired woman stood there. Her blue eyes shone through the dim. I held my breath.

"Joe," she said. It sounded like the way you would greet someone you had been waiting for for a long time.

"Sasha." I'd never heard Joe's voice like that. So serious and quiet, deeper than usual.

"You've come," she said. Her tone was low and a little rough. I wanted to fall under its spell—let it lead me into a dark place where I could find who I was, but part of me did not want to know. I grew suddenly so weary, as if the forest were a dream weighing down on me, pressing me into sleep. I closed my eyes.

When I woke I was lying on a small cot in a darkened room.

I sat up. "Joey?"

There was silence. Then a woman's voice said, "He had to go back. I told him you'd be safe here."

She came toward me. She was wearing a floor-length silvery nightgown and her hair was the same, almost metallic in the candlelight. She had long, sinewy arms, strong arms. I looked at her hands. The middle finger stretched out beyond the others just like mine.

"I'm Sasha," she said. "You're Liv."

I nodded.

"We've been waiting for you."

We? Who else was there? I looked around the room. The walls were made of rough-hewn logs. There was a large, soft deerskin rug on the floor. Besides the bed there were very few furnishings. Who was "we," where were they and why had they been waiting?

As if she heard my thought, she answered it with a similar question. "Why did you want to find me?"

There was a reason, some reason, but I couldn't think of it.

"How do you know Joey?" I asked because I didn't have an answer for her. A question followed by a question followed by a question.

"We've known each other since I moved to town." Her blue eyes were rimmed with dark lashes; it looked as if she had elaborate eyeliner on or it could have been natural. She touched her hair gently, where the silver caught the light. "I would have had him bring you to me sooner but it wasn't the time yet. You've been doing well so far but things are going to get harder now."

I wrapped my arms around myself. It was dark outside; my mother would worry. I patted my pocket for my cell phone and took it out. She'd called. Corey had, too, probably. I wanted to reassure them and, in doing so, to reassure myself that I was okay, that I hadn't lost my mind.

"I have to get home."

"Yes, I know," the woman said. Sasha. That was her name. "But there is something I need to tell you."

I wasn't ready; whatever it was, I wasn't ready. I looked away. I stood up. "I'm not sure I can find my way home."

"My boys will take you," Sasha said. "Later. We need to talk." She reached out her hand and I saw the long middle finger again like an accusation. She parted her lips and I saw her small, sharp white teeth.

Suddenly I was so afraid I could hardly breathe.

I stood up and went to the door. She followed me. I heard her make a sound, a soft howling noise. The night was as silvery as her hair, an almost full moon so bright that even through the thick trees it shone. I looked at the woman with the long fingers and the sharp teeth and I started to run.

I didn't know where I was going. I kept running, though, wanting to get out of the wood; it wasn't a safe place anymore. It held the secret to who I was and I didn't want it now.

As I ran I heard footsteps behind me. They grew faster. The footsteps caught up and then they were all around me. Fear slammed my chest. They would take me down, these creatures. They would eat me alive. I would be the next one dead. My father would find my eviscerated body and try to solve the case. Was the moon full? It was almost full. It would be full the next night.

But then I was running with the footsteps, not away. They did not catch me. They surrounded me in a pack and led me on.

The footsteps belonged to men, seven young men with dark hair and pale golden eyes that flashed in the dark. A surge of freedom leaped in my chest as I kept pace with them. They were fast, like me, strong, like me. Sometimes one would look back and smile whitely at me with Sasha's small, sharp teeth. I wondered if I was dreaming. I felt my heartbeat in my feet as if my center was low to the ground and the earth was guiding me.

We reached the edge of the forest. I heard soft laughter, the snap of branches. I stopped, bent over, panting, out of breath.

When I looked up the boys were standing there, watching me.

My brothers, I thought.

And I was relieved. And terrified.

I recognized them from before; I had seen them all before.

It was at the party where Carl Olaf kissed me. They were the boys I had seen on the road; I had never forgotten them. I had dreamed about them, too, especially the tallest one, the one who had looked back at me that night. About once a year I had a dream that he was in my bedroom, pawing through the diary I always kept by my bed. One morning I woke up to find it open, though I didn't remember leaving it like that.

The tallest boy, the one who had looked back, came forward and held out his hand. When I extended mine tentatively he took it and kissed it. I could feel the heat of his lips even after he had moved his mouth away.

"This is Victor," said one of them, a slightly smaller version of the first. "I am Sebastian."

A thinner boy danced forward, grinning, and took my hand next. "Felix."

"Hello," I said.

Sebastian said, "Marcos," and a broadly built

boy nodded his head at me.

Sebastian said, "Gregory and Frederick," and identical boys also nodded.

The smallest boy, who looked a lot like a smiling Victor, shook my hand vigorously. "I'm Amorus."

I smiled a little. Part of me wanted to pat his head.

Then Victor turned and the others turned with him, curving their spines around slowly until they faced the trees. He stopped and looked back at me. "I have been waiting for years to be formally introduced to you, Olivia," he said. "You are a rare thing. We are at your service." Then he was gone.

I had been mystified by this boy before, when he had seemed to read my mind on the road four years ago, mystified enough to continue dreaming about him, even though I had tried to forget him. Now he had found me, and he had remembered me, or at least it seemed that way, by what he had said about being formally introduced. But what did he mean—*rare thing*—and why was he at my service? He was beautiful and interested in me, which should have been enough to make me want to find out more, at the very least, but instead I wished I had never seen him.

He was connected to danger.

But, as it turned out, danger was everywhere.

When I got home my father was on the porch, waiting for me. He stood slowly as I approached and I saw the black outline of his football shoulders against the yellow porch light.

"Where you been?" he asked me. His voice was deep and I could hear the liquor slurring it. My hands instinctively went to my throat. It was hard to speak.

I slowed down and walked up the front path with my head lowered.

"We tried calling you. You know you have to be home by eight."

I nodded and kept my eyes on the ground.

"We called McIntyre. He didn't know where you were either." His breath smelled like booze and he stood shakily, leaning against the door frame.

"I'm sorry," I said. "I went to the woods and I fell asleep." I was at the door now and I just wanted to go inside and lie down but he blocked my way.

"Worried sick," he said. "Your mother was. I'll tell you what, I almost called my men out. You want to get torn to shreds like all those others? Next time I'll drag your ass with me to see the autopsy. They don't even look human."

I put my hand on the doorknob. He was drunk; his reflexes might be off.

But no. I saw him raise his hand to strike and I cringed but I couldn't move away. His hand came down hard against my cheekbone. Tears sprang into my eyes and the damp light was sprinkled with black dots.

"Get your ass in there," he said. "You're shit out of luck if you think I'm going to let you wander around like this again." I felt him watching me the way he did when he was mad, his eyes narrowed at my back as I headed for the stairs.

"What the hell are you anyway?" I heard him mumble into the darkness. "You aren't mine, that's for sure. You never were."

He was right to ask. I didn't know what I was. Or what had happened to me in the woods or why the beautiful boy, Victor, had any interest in being formally introduced to me. This last was flattering but it also scared me. Everything scared me. And now my father had hit me in the face. I suppressed the desire to turn to him, bare my teeth and growl. Spittle accumulated in the corners of my mouth. I gripped the banister and forced my feet to walk up the steps to my room. When I got there I took my last Xanax. Nieberding had given them to me for the times when things got heavy, when the Lexapro wasn't enough.

Until it worked, I wrote, over and over in my diary, the words to a prayer I'd made up: "May the river of peace flow through me. May the winds of calm blow anger from my mind. May love's fire burn away my pain. May the great mother protect me and may I know how to protect her as I go." I said it every night before I went to bed. This time I needed it more than ever—something to ward off whatever was coming on.

I couldn't let myself get angry. I couldn't allow it. I stopped writing the words and gripped the sheets.

May the winds of calm blow anger from my mind.

The meds slowly started to work until very little mattered anymore except sleep.

In the morning I checked my cell phone messages. There were five calls from my mom, one from Pace and three from Corey. I rolled over in bed and lightly touched my cheek where it stung. I knew it would be purple in a few hours if it wasn't already. *May the river of peace flow through me. . . .*

I got up and went to take my Lexapro but I was out. *Damn.* The phone vibrated in my hand, like a live thing, as I held it. Corey.

"Hey," I said. "I'm sorry you couldn't reach me."

"Where were you?" His voice sounded higher, shaky.

"I went into the woods and I fell asleep," I said. "I guess I was more tired than I thought." It sounded lame, even to me.

"That's f'ed up, Liv. I kept calling you. You can't just go out there by yourself and sleep! It's not safe."

"I know. I'm sorry." I felt tears making the ducts in the corner of my eyes tingle. "Don't be mad at me."

"I was *worried!*"

"I know. I just mean . . . my dad already . . ."

"What?" I could feel Corey's whole body tense, just from the sound of his voice.

"Never mind. I have to go now. I'm already late for work." My fingers gingerly explored the swelling on the side of my face again. At least no one would question it at work. Only Corey, Joe and Pace would care at all.

"Liv! I need to see you!"

"Okay, okay," I said. "Today after work. Meet me in the woods."

I was exhausted by the time I met Corey. My face hurt and I felt slightly feverish as I stepped from the air-conditioned ice cream parlor out into the heat. By the time I got to the woods I just wanted to lie down and sleep for hours.

Corey took me by the shoulders and examined my face. He touched my cheek gently.

"What happened?"

I shook my head, turned my face away and reached for his hand. We walked in among the trees. I tried to remember which way the cabin was but I had no idea. It really seemed as if I'd dreamed the whole thing, but then a lot of my life felt that way.

We sat by the creek in the dim light and I kicked off my shoes and leaned against his chest. I was so relieved to be with him, here in the quiet. His heart was thumping. I traced my fingers along his bare forearm where the skin was satiny smooth and the veins pushed up slightly under the surface.

"Tell me what happened," he said. "Tell me why you didn't call me."

"I told you. I fell asleep."

"Liv, that's bullshit. You don't go alone into the woods where four people got whacked and lie down and sleep. And what happened to your face?"

"My dad," I said. "He was drinking."

Corey drew away and balled a fistful of dried leaves in his hand. "I'm going to kill him."

"Shhh. Don't say that. Kiss it."

He bent down and pressed his mouth lightly to the bruise. I could feel the imprint of his lips on my cheek, warm and soft with tiny lines running over the surface.

He kept kissing me, moving toward my mouth. I turned my lips up to his and gasped as he ran his tongue lightly over them.

"Corey . . ."

He hushed me with more kisses. I knew I couldn't do this. Not today. I wouldn't be able to stop myself— maybe not. After what had happened in the cabin and then with my dad I didn't feel in control at all.

May the river of peace flow through me. . . .

Corey put his hands in my hair, stroked my face and neck. His fingers hesitated, lingered above my breasts. I sighed and my chest lifted against his touch as if my heart were trying to get closer to him. He slid his hand up my T-shirt and fumbled with my bra. It came unclasped and warmth radiated from his hand, through the center of my back and out into my limbs. He smoothed both hands down over my hips and I wriggled in his arms so that my back was pressed against his chest and my hips to his groin. Then he reached down into my jeans and I arched my back and turned my head so that our mouths found each other again. My teeth caught his lower lip and I wanted to bite down and taste the salt sea of his blood. I wanted to take off all my clothes and take off all his clothes and nuzzle his neck, nip his chin, bat him with my paws, lick him with my tongue, our loins locked together, my tail raised, brushing against him . . .

I sat up. "I can't."

"What? Why not, Liv?" He was breathing hard.

"I thought we decided . . ."

"We've been together for years."

I put my face in my hands. "I know."

"I'm freaking out, here, Liv. First you disappear. Then you tell me your dad is beating on you."

"I'm sorry!" I was shouting now.

Corey stood up. "At least explain it to me."

"I can't," I said. "I don't understand myself. It just doesn't feel . . . safe."

"What are you talking about?" he asked. "I've never been with anyone else. I have a condom. I always bring a goddamn condom."

"I know, Corey. I'm sorry. But don't . . . don't make me mad."

I could feel the moon swelling in the sky beyond

the trees. There was too much saliva in my mouth and my teeth ached. My jaw felt like it was cracking, more teeth trying to burst through the surface of my tender gums. My hips ached, too, in that strange way, as if the joints were loosening, the bones elongating. Something was happening and I couldn't push it away anymore.

Once my mother had called me over to the computer. She had showed me some pictures online of dogs and sheep ripped apart, bloody carcasses with chunks ripped out, down to the bone. She wanted to convince me that killing the wolf hadn't been wrong. Suddenly I understood why those pictures made me want to die, and it wasn't just that they made me think of what I'd heard about the deaths of Reed, Louden, Dan and Bob. Evisceration. Carnage. That was me. That was what I was and what I could do.

I staggered to my feet and pushed Corey away with my hand on his chest.

"What are you doing?" Corey was staring at me

in a way I'd never seen him look before. It was like he didn't recognize me. I had to get out of there fast.

I turned and ran away from him, then, into the forest to find the ones who were just as brutal and dangerous as I was.

I ran and ran. The forest thundered with sounds around me. My ears twitched and turned. I could hear every leaf crackle, every insect move its wings. The smells overwhelmed me, too—rotting plants and small animal carcasses under the sweeter fragrance of summer growth. The fading light flashed through the dark branches and I kept running until the darkness was everywhere. I could feel the pull of the hot summer moon though it hadn't fully risen yet. I could feel every root and pebble under my bare feet.

My feet . . .

I looked down and saw that they were covered with hair. I fell forward onto my hands and my hips and back arched, stretched out, lowered to the ground.

Everything ached with a fierce pull. My head ached as if my skull was stretching out, using all the energy in my body. Weakness permeated my cells. When had I eaten last? The thought of the ice cream at work made my stomach clench.

Somewhere nearby I caught a familiar scent. *My brothers*, I thought without reason. *My mother.*

Just as I thought it I felt something grip my shoulder. But my shoulder was lower and smaller, not really a human shoulder at all.

It is time for you to hear the story, she said.

The Curse

I lay beside my brothers on the floor of the cabin. They smelled of leaves and moonlight. The closeness of their bodies comforted me now. I no longer wanted to avoid what they were, what I was. I felt a certain relief, the relief of surrender, even to something dangerous. The dangerous thing had happened—I didn't have to fight it anymore—and, at last, someone was going to explain it to me.

In front of me was a slab of freshly killed meat, still steaming. Deer. I tore into it with my sharp teeth. It buzzed with recently faded life. The weak feeling went away. My mouth was dripping with blood, rich and strong as liquid iron.

The moon was rising outside the cabin window above the trees. Through the glass and the scaffolding of dark branches it was huge and white and completely round.

Sasha sat in front of us. Her silver fur shone. Her eyes shone, too, in the pale light.

Are you all right? she asked after I had finished my meal. *Asked* may not be the right word; she made sounds—a soft, low, throaty groan—and I understood them.

I swept my rough tongue gingerly over my arm. But it wasn't an arm anymore. The hair tickled my mouth. I wasn't entirely myself and yet I wasn't all that different. I wished there was a mirror so I could see, but part of me didn't want to.

I have to tell you now, Sasha said. *It is time. You will be going away soon.*

I have to get home. I wasn't really speaking either but

that is what I communicated to her. *My dad . . .*

He won't hurt you this time.

How did she know? She didn't know him. I lowered my head.

As if she could read my thoughts, she said, *It would be worse for him to see you like this. We'll make sure you are safe.*

I looked at the pack of young wolves surrounding me. They were fierce and strong with thick fur and golden eyes. Victor, Sebastian, Felix, Marcos, Gregory, Frederick and Amorus. I now understood that they lived here as young men most of the time—the men I had seen on the road after the party and again last night—until they became animals. They watched their mother carefully.

I'm not going away soon, I told her.

I think you will, when everything comes to a head.

What do you mean? How do you know all these things? Who are you?

I am the daughter of Ivan, the one your mother killed from the helicopter with her father, Sasha said. *He was the largest and the strongest of them all. Everyone loved him. He and my mother, Elena, were inseparable.*

Ivan was running through the snow when she shot him from her helicopter. She shot him again and again. The snow was stained with blood.

After his death Elena used the curse. She had never resorted to it before. It can destroy the lives of everyone it touches. But Elena felt she had no choice. She came to your grandfather one night and told him but he pretended not to hear her, pretended she was a dream. But none of it was a dream. You are the result.

Of your mother's curse? I asked.

Sasha nodded.

I looked down at my body. Of course. I was a curse. That was all I was.

Sasha went on: *You were born cursed but your mother didn't know. Your grandfather could have told her but he didn't and she probably wouldn't have listened anyway. Some years later my mother was dying. She called Peter and me to her bedside and told us to go kill your mother. The curse wasn't enough. She wanted the ultimate revenge.*

My mother killed your father. Your mother wanted to kill my mother. I didn't pose these as questions. It was clear to me, as if I'd heard it all before.

Yes.

Who is Peter?

Sasha turned her head away and stared into the darkness. Her eyes glowed brighter. *Peter was my husband,* she said. *He's gone now.*

What happened to him? I asked, dreading the answer.

Peter, Sasha said, *was killed, too.*

I heard a low growl come from the large wolf beside me. Victor.

I shook my head. *I don't want to hear it.*

Yes. By your mother. Four years ago. We had come looking for her and he couldn't get close enough to do what we had to do. She wore the silver cross. Sasha shivered violently. *And she shot him.*

I could see the dead wolf in the back of my mother's truck. I could see him as clearly as if he were bleeding to death in front of my eyes. But he wasn't a wolf. He was what I was.

That was when I changed, I said.

Sasha nodded. *I know,* she told me. *I was there. And now you have changed again.*

Why? Why has it only happened twice? I felt like it was going to happen more than that but it didn't.

It's different for everyone but for most of us it's connected to powerful emotions, Sasha said. *For female shape-shifters there is also the menses factor. And the moon, of course. These things have to be working in concert. The rage can be controlled in various ways but not the other things, obviously.*

Shape-shifters? You mean . . .

Lycanthropy.

Werewolves? I had read books and seen movies and TV shows about them. I knew that they changed during the full moon, that they could be destroyed with silver. It couldn't be true—they weren't real—but if it was true then suddenly everything made sense. All the memories I had tried to keep at a distance, repress, send back to the dark place where they had come from rushed back at me. The wolf in the truck. The smell of blood. The hair on my body. The pull of the moon.

The rage in my soul.

Sasha nodded. *But I prefer to call it the frenzy. One can be born that way or one can be cursed.*

So my mother had done this to me somehow. My mother had looked out across the pale terrain that winter over seventeen years ago, seen the wolf in its freedom and in its glory, and she had shot that wolf down. And because of this I had been cursed. All the weirdness about me, all the wildness and the violence that my mother sensed and hated, and that I feared and hated, too—all that was her fault. It was as if she had put it all on me without realizing it so that she could appear pure to the world, an angel. My mother had denied every dark part of herself and here was Sasha who lived it out in each breath of forest air and each bite of bloody meat.

And what am I supposed to do now? I yelped. *I'm a monster. I can't even tell my boyfriend what I am. My mother doesn't know what she did. My father hits me.*

I heard Victor growl again. *He won't anymore.* Victor

almost sounded, what? Protective? I didn't understand why he cared. What interest could he have in me?

Sasha came and knelt beside me, nuzzled my face with hers. I closed my eyes, entranced, letting myself be soothed and comforted in that moment. My pulse slowed. There was a long silence. I opened my eyes and looked up at her.

Then:

Kill your mother, she whispered.

Kill her? My mother? My *mother*? Who was this thing instructing me to do this? Who was Sasha and why had I allowed her to speak to me, how had I ever imagined that I could be hers? The hair on my body pricked up as I thought about the deaths in the woods, the way the woods I loved were so full of so much violent death. And that is where Sasha lived.

As cold and detached as my mother could be, at least she loved me; she was human. Sasha was an animal. But I *had* wanted to kill my mother. Maybe I was more like Sasha than I knew.

Even though I now understood more about what had happened to me, I still didn't fully understand the consequences of what I was.

I didn't want to understand. I wanted to escape. I stretched my spine and stood shakily; my legs were stiff. I shook them out and pawed the ground until I could smell the murky, mineral sustenance of the earth and then, with that, I ran.

Help

When I got home at dawn it was my mother who was waiting for me. She sat on the porch wrapped in a robe. She had her glasses on and there were pastel foam curlers in her hair.

My mother didn't look like someone who would hurt anyone, not even a wolf. And she certainly didn't look like anyone I would ever want to hurt.

I, on the other hand, must have looked hideous because she gasped and stood up when she saw me.

Then I realized. I was naked and shivering. I stopped in my tracks, trying to cover my chest and between my legs as best I could. There was blood on my mouth and hands. Memories of the night came rushing back to me and I felt like vomiting.

"What happened?" she said. "Who did this to you?"

I couldn't even begin to tell her any of it, or even let myself acknowledge it. "I'm okay, Mom. No one hurt me."

She ran down the steps, taking off her bathrobe as she went, and wrapped me in it. She was wearing striped pajamas underneath. We went inside.

"We need to get you to a hospital," she said.

"No. I'm really fine."

"Liv, you are not fine!" She was reaching for the phone and I stopped her.

"I was at a girlfriend's," I said.

"Girlfriend? You haven't had a girlfriend for years. Who is this girlfriend?"

I ignored her.

"We were swimming at this party and some boys

stole our clothes. And they . . . locked us out."

"Locked you out? Of where?"

"Where the party was. I was afraid to come home and get hit again."

She touched my mouth gently. "This is blood, Olivia. I'm telling your father."

"No!" I pulled away from her and tried to calm down. "Listen. Mom." My teeth were chattering so much that it was hard to talk. "I had a hard night. But I'm okay. No one hurt me. Except Dad last night."

She put her hand on my arm and I jerked it away automatically, then, when I saw her eyes, regretted it.

"I'm sorry he did that," she said. "He loses control when he's drinking. But you need to learn that you just can't go AWOL on us. Not in a place where things . . . happen."

"What do you mean where things *happen*?" I asked defensively.

"You know what. I'm talking about the murders in the woods. There's a reason we're protective."

"Mom," I began, but I didn't even know what I was going to say. I was so tired I could barely stand.

"We need to get you some help."

"Help" came the next day, in the form of an exam by the family doctor (proving I had not been molested or physically injured in any way and, luckily, not revealing anything else abnormal about me) and a visit to Dr. Nieberding. He fell back into the reclining chair as he always did, as if that motion and the sound it made signaled the beginning of his fifty-minute hour.

"So, Olivia, do you know why you are here this time?" he asked me.

"Liv," I said. "It's still Liv."

"Do you know why you're here, Liv?"

I shrugged and looked past him out the window, wanting to escape to the forest. There was a small tree in the courtyard of Nieberding's building. I imagined that it was dreaming of the woods, too.

"Do you think that you might have some new

issues that need to be addressed? Some things that you feel you can't express at home?"

I picked at my cuticles. "Not really."

"Your mother still feels that this condition of yours is affecting your self-esteem."

I folded my arms in my lap to hide the hair.

"Would you say that is accurate?" he asked.

I needed sarcasm to keep him at a distance. What if he got me to reveal too much? "The hirsuteness? Because you can just come right out and say it."

"She thinks you might have internalized it even more than before. She says some of your behavior has seemed almost . . . animalistic."

What if they knew? They would never believe it but what if they knew something? "Like what?" I asked warily.

"She told me you didn't come home last night. Until the morning. And without your clothes? You seemed to imitate some of the qualities of a . . . well, a wild animal."

I tensed in my chair. "My mother has a tendency to exaggerate," I said.

"You sound angry at your mother. Would you say that is accurate?"

I shrugged and looked at my shoes.

"Have you been taking your medication? Do you think this may have something to do with the behavior?"

I had to change the subject. "I'm angry. Yes. I stayed out once one night and my father hit me in the face. Then I stayed out again because of that and my mother decides I'm an animal and need treatment."

"Your father hit you?"

"He has before." Besides that last incident there was the time when I turned thirteen and my mother killed the wolf. When I came back from the woods my father smacked me hard across the mouth. But I didn't mind it so much that time. I almost welcomed it as punishment for the thoughts I'd had about my mother. It didn't make me mad or make me frenzy again; I only hung my head that time.

The doctor made a note on his pad. I resisted the impulse to snarl at him and lick my chops. He continued to ask me questions about my parents, my friends, starting school in the fall. I evaded everything. I was thinking about Corey and part of me wanted to talk about him, just to be able to get it out, but I knew I couldn't say a thing to this doctor person. Corey and I hadn't spoken since our argument the day before when I had run away from him. We usually saw each other, or at least spoke, every day.

Nieberding asked me more about the night before and I told him the same story I'd given my mom, emphasizing the fact that I was afraid to come home because I thought my father would hit me again. The doctor warned me about the dangers of the woods, of being out in this town alone at night. Finally the session was over.

"I'm afraid we'll have to stop now," Nieberding said, as he always did, with a touch of condescending concern in his voice, as if I'd be upset.

I stood and curtsied.

"Watch out for your sheep and chickens, good Doctor," I said.

I couldn't resist.

When I got home I lay in a fetal position on my bed, holding my cell phone, not even able to write in my diary, trying to send Corey a psychic message to call me back. I had tried him repeatedly since that morning but he hadn't answered. My heart actually felt like a hard thing that had cracked, almost like a broken rib, and every breath seemed to make the pain worse.

It was terrible not talking to Corey. I wasn't complete anymore without him. I really felt like a part of me had been severed and all my blood was draining out through the place where the part had been. And so much had happened; it was hard to handle it alone. Not that I was ready to tell anyone yet.

When the phone rang I gasped for breath but it wasn't Corey. It was Pace. He sounded about the way I felt.

"What's wrong?"

"I was going to ask you the same question," Pace said.

We both just sat there silently. Then he spoke.

"I need your help."

I still hadn't heard from Corey when I met Pace the next day after work at the Fairborn house on Green. He was sitting on the carved front porch in the shadows with his head down. D'Argenton, the Great Dane mix from the pound, was sniffing his ear. I went and sat next to them. The heat in the air was almost unbearable, like you wanted to run screaming from it. Sweat trickled down my neck.

"What happened?" I realized how much had changed for me since I'd talked to Pace last and I felt bad that I hadn't called him before. I'd been trying to focus on Corey and deal with all the weird shit that had gone down but I'd neglected my friend.

He looked up at me and his eyes were rimmed with red. "It so makes fucking sense."

"What? Pace, what?"

He crossed his arms over his chest and clutched at his shoulders, rocked gently back and forth.

I grabbed his bicep. "What is it?"

"I'm losing my mind. I must be losing my goddamn mind."

"Okay, start at the beginning." It felt like the first time in days I wasn't fixated on my own problems. Pace looked like he was going to start sobbing any second.

"I can't talk about it."

"Is it something with the guy? Michael?"

Pace stopped and stared at me, like he was pleading with me to make it better. "I feel insane. Am I going insane, Liv? Will they lock me up again?"

"It's okay. Everything will be okay," I told him.

"You're not crazy." But what did I know? I was crazy myself, it seemed. I'd just been told that I was a lycanthrope. D'Argenton started to whine softly and I stroked his long haunch, as much to comfort myself as to quiet him.

Pace looked back toward the house. The arched windows were dark and reminded me of giant eyes raising their brows at us. I remembered the terrible cold inside there. It would have been refreshing today, if it didn't make you feel like throwing up. That kind of cold wasn't natural.

"Do you want me to go inside with you?" I asked.

Pace stood up. "No. I want to get the hell out of here. I never want to come back."

I stood, too, and walked with him up the path. D'Argenton followed regally behind us.

"Or maybe I do want to stay," he said, looking back at the house that was looming up darker in the gathering twilight. "Maybe I want to stay here forever."

"What is that supposed to mean? Pace?"

We stood facing each other on the sidewalk in front of the house. It was eerily quiet and Pace seemed far away in his thoughts.

"I'm worried," I told him.

"Never mind," he said, and I didn't press him. I let him brush me off even though an uneasy stirring in my belly told me I shouldn't have.

Pace's gaze focused back on me and I recognized the friend I knew. "Come walk with me. *You* don't look okay." He put his arm around me and I almost started crying.

"Corey hasn't called me. We had a fight."

Pace squeezed my shoulder. "Jesus. What's happening here? If you guys can't get along, no one can."

"We don't have to talk about me."

"Yes, we do. What did you fight about?"

"No, Pace. Forget it. I'm really worried about you."

"I'll be okay." He pulled his T-shirt up to wipe the sweat from his face. His abs showed, perfectly cut. He did thousands of sit-ups a day, it looked like.

Pace seemed perfect in every way although I knew he wasn't. I never knew all the details of why he was hospitalized. I wondered if maybe he'd tried to hurt himself back then.

Pace didn't want to go home, so after he dropped D'Argenton off he stayed for dinner that night. When we'd eaten, or sufficiently picked at food in my case, Pace and I went to my room and lay on my bed and I told him more about Corey and me, how I was afraid if we had sex something bad might happen. Pace kept encouraging me, telling me it was obvious that Corey loved me and that it would be a beautiful thing and that he wished he had such a great boyfriend. But he seemed weary and distracted and I couldn't bring myself to tell him about the frenzy and why I was really afraid to make love to Corey. I wanted to ask Pace more about Michael but his eyes had a panicked look when I tried to bring it up again so I dropped the subject and let him go on about how I should sleep with Corey. This made everything worse for me. I wanted my boyfriend so badly by the time Pace left that I felt as if I were going to climb out of my skin.

I picked up my phone and texted Corey.

meet me at haunted house on green please i am so sorry i need you love liv

I didn't even wait to hear back from him, just climbed out the window, scaled down the wall and started running.

When I got to the house I still hadn't heard from him and he wasn't waiting for me. I went up to the door—it was locked. I rattled the doorknob anyway and all of a sudden it opened, as if someone had unlocked it. The wicked cold hit me again and I wished I had brought a sweater but the night had felt so warm. The furniture looked like ghosts hunkered down around the room and there was a strong musty smell. Walls creaked and popped with noise around me.

"Corey," I said softly into the darkness, just to comfort myself with the sound of his name; I didn't really believe he would be there. Then I added, "Michael?"

Someone grabbed me and I screamed and whipped my head around.

It was Corey.

"You scared the hell out of me!" I shouted at him.

"I'm sorry, Liv, but you picked this place to meet."

Then I looked into his eyes and my sadness and relief at not having seen him took over. I fell into his arms and started crying. His familiar scent and warmth calmed me down almost immediately. I stopped shivering and closed my eyes, pressing my damp face into his chest. He led me out of the house and we sat on the porch behind the fir trees.

"That house is messed up," he said. "Why's it so cold?"

"Maybe it really is haunted."

"Like me." Corey glanced at me sideways.

"What?" I'd lost the thread of conversation so I just stared at him.

"I can't stop thinking about you."

"Me, too," I said. "You."

"It sucks."

"I know. Listen, Corey, I'm sorry. I wanted to apologize."

He nodded but he wouldn't look me in the eye.

"The reason I didn't make love with you isn't because I don't want to. And it's not because I'm scared for the reasons you think." A flood of relief washed over me; I was going to be able to share my secret. . . .

"What is it? You know you can tell me anything. I've known you forever."

I reached out and touched his arm. A jolt of electricity went through me and I had to move my hand away.

"I'm afraid I'm a monster," I said. "And that if we make love something bad might happen because of that."

"What do you mean 'a monster'?"

I struggled for the words but they stuck in my throat like a piece of poison apple. I couldn't do it. I couldn't tell him.

"Just . . . that . . . I wouldn't do it right or . . ."

"Liv!" He stopped me, grabbed my hand, and I surrendered to the electric currents pulsing through my body. "This is me here you're talking to. What are you going on about, crazy girl?"

"I know. I'm sorry." I lowered my head. "Can we get out of here?"

I gripped his hand tighter and we stood up and began to walk silently away from the cold house and toward the woods. I didn't feel giddy or even filled with the usual desire. I felt serious, as if we were embarking on a journey—something sacred. I knew I wanted to be with Corey but I was also afraid. I still hadn't been able to tell him the truth. I had trusted him with everything but this.

As if he could read my thoughts, he said, "There's

nothing to be scared of, Liv. We love each other. That's what matters, right?"

It was true. And I wanted to believe that was all that mattered.

Love

Corey had a flashlight and he shone it along the path, a pale flicker of comfort, as we went deeper into the trees. We'd taken this path so many times before as children, really, even though we thought we were grown up, holding hands like kids in a fairy tale, safe—from whatever mystery lurked in the dark—only because we had each other. Now I knew one thing that lurked in the dark and it was me. But at that moment I was safe from that, too.

We lay down by the creek on a patch of mossy ground among some roots. Corey made a pillow for me with his sweatshirt. Our bodies were almost the same length and size, his legs just a little longer and hips just a little narrower. We lay on our sides, looking at each other, our hands entwined. I loved the pale color of my skin against the warm glow of his. Corey's eyes shone in the darkness like the eyes of an animal and for a moment I thought he was like me, too, but then he kissed me and I knew it was just desire that had changed him.

They say it will hurt. It didn't hurt, maybe because of what my body had already been through when I changed. In spite of my initial fear, it felt like I was safe, completely safe.

They say it will be short the first time. It wasn't short. Just because Corey had waited so long didn't mean he had to make it happen all at once. Our bodies took their time.

They say you will lose yourself. It wasn't true. I felt as if I had finally found myself and the girl in Corey's arms wasn't a monster, not at all.

The only problem was I couldn't feel it entirely. They say that's a side effect of the meds I take. It was okay, I was still happy to be with Corey, but it was like the lower half of my body wasn't quite all the way there, like it maybe even belonged to someone else. For the first time I wondered about going off the Lexapro. Maybe I didn't need that anymore. *Maybe now that Corey and I made love,* I thought in my euphoric state, *maybe I won't be as susceptible to changing. Maybe I'm cured,* I imagined as I drifted in and out of a dream.

Afterward Corey's eyes turned soft and calm again and he snuggled me in his arms.

If you saw us you would have thought we were just a boy and girl who had loved each other for a long time and finally made love—just a normal boy and girl who had waited what might be considered abnormally long. That's how I felt until I got home that night.

But later, as I lay in my bed, looking at the hair on my body, I remembered that we weren't normal.

Corey and I could never be. He was a boy and I was a monster. I knew that even though I hadn't turned into a wolf when we made love, even though I loved him more than anyone on earth, I could possibly still hurt him; he was not my kind. My kind waited for me in the woods. And they had a task they wanted me to perform, one I couldn't do.

Early the next morning I called Pace. He sounded small and hoarse.

"I went by the house," I said.

"Yeah?"

I could tell by the tight sound of his voice that he didn't want me to talk about it. Maybe he didn't want to think about Michael but I wondered if it might be good for him to talk about it anyway.

"It felt really creepy there."

He was quiet on the other end, for an uncomfortably long amount of time. Then he said, "Did you go inside?" There was so much tension in the way he asked and I knew he meant, *Was Michael there?*

"No one was there. It was really cold in a way I can't explain. I felt sick to my stomach."

"Me, too," he said. "Sick."

"Why, do you think? They say it's haunted so . . ."

Pace cut me off. "I don't want to talk about it," he said. He was quiet for a moment, then he added, "Tell me about you. Have you talked to Corey?"

"We saw each other last night," I said.

"You made up?"

I didn't want to make Pace feel worse but I needed to share what had happened, the beauty of it, like he'd said, and the fears that I still had. "More than that."

"You had sex?"

"Yes."

"How was it?"

"It was great," I said.

"You don't sound entirely great."

"Neither do you." I suddenly really heard the sadness thickening his words. "Are you okay?"

"Oh, yeah. Everything's cool."

I wasn't sure it was true so I asked if he wanted me to come over after work.

"No, it's all right. I just want to be alone right now."

"Are you sure?" I asked, but, again, I didn't push him. I had so much on my mind. I had learned why I was what I was, what it was called. I had made love to Corey but not told him what I was.

I had met my pack and they wanted me to kill my own mother.

"Love is a werewolf," I wrote in my diary after Pace left. "Influenced by the moon and terror. And always about to change. Romantic love can blind you, too, just the way I could become blinded by the curse of the animal inside. It can make you neglect what is most important at the time."

Brothers

Victor is the oldest. He is the biggest and strongest, the most handsome, the leader. His eyes are fierce and he rarely speaks. He is the one who I had noticed first on the road that night, and who I had never been able to forget.

Sebastian is second. He is more shy and gentle and follows Victor around, waiting for instructions from his brother.

Felix is third. He is quick and light, a prankster, always in motion.

Marcos, fourth, is heavyset and serious.

Gregory and Frederick are the twins. They stay to themselves and communicate to each other without words.

Amorus is the baby, a small version of Victor but less brooding.

These are my wolf brothers. The night after I made love with Corey I woke to a soft howling sound, like wind in my ear, and saw seven pairs of eyes watching me from the dark corners of my room.

"Come with us," Victor said. "Come run with us."

I pulled the sheets around me. I was only wearing a boy's undershirt and panties.

"I can't," I said.

"You don't have to be afraid," said Felix.

I closed my eyes tight like a child who thinks she can make the monsters go away if she just doesn't look at them. It got very silent. I couldn't even hear a breath, except my own. But when I opened my eyes they were all still there.

Amorus approached me. He was a little younger

than me with big, sweet eyes. He put out his hand and lightly pawed my knee under the sheet, cocked his head to the side.

"What do you want?" I said into the darkness where the rest of them waited.

"We want to help you. We want to teach you about what you are." It was Victor's voice again. He came up behind Amorus and put his hand on his little brother's shoulder, ruffled the top of Amorus's head with his chin.

"Sasha told me to kill my mother," I said. "How do I know you won't do that?" I looked around at the eyes glowing in the darkness. "She's my *mother!*"

"Sometimes Sasha gets carried away," Victor said softly. "We don't want to hurt your mother. We couldn't anyway. She's safe from us."

"Safe!" I could feel my fear turning to anger. The hairs prickled up on my arms. "I'm not safe from you! There are seven men in my bedroom!"

Victor motioned for Sebastian to come forward. He stood behind his brother as Sebastian spoke. "Not seven men, sister. Seven unarmed wolves. And your daddy sleeps with a shotgun under the bed. And your mother never takes off her silver cross."

I closed my eyes again, put my hands over my ears and shook my head from side to side to make the dream go away. But it wasn't a dream. They were all still there when I opened my eyes.

Scoot finally heard them. He was scratching at my door, whining and barking.

Victor was staring at me. He made a gesture with his head for me to follow him, went to the window and disappeared. One by one each brother did the same.

I sat frozen in my bed. What the hell had just happened? I realized I was holding my breath and I gasped for air. Then I went to the window and peeked out. They were huddled on the grass looking up at me, except for Victor who had turned away, facing the woods. I could run with my brothers; my legs were already tingling with the sensation of freedom.

I could smell the night, feed on it. It would course through me; I would be a part of it. I would run and play and feast on flesh, get drunk on blood all night with seven beautiful young men.

But Corey? He would look into my eyes the next time I saw him and sense that I had moved further away, become even less like him.

Yes, Corey. I'm a werewolf. I thirst after human blood and I run all night with a pack of seven males. I could kill you if I wanted. Rage lives inside of me, waiting to come out in the shape of a monster.

I could betray Corey and be true to a part of my nature or I could choose not to. Corey was right, though I chose to ignore it; we were different. I was much wilder.

I shivered, got back in bed, pulled the covers over my head and began to scribble furiously in my diary.

"Liv," called the night, "Liv."

I ignored her.

July

After that night I tried to shut out everything except for Corey. I figured if I stayed focused on him and the joy we could give to each other nothing else could hurt me. If I were careful I wouldn't have to deal with my father's anger or my mother's fear. I wouldn't have to think about Sasha and what she wanted me to do and what she wanted to do herself but couldn't. I could just go to work serving ice cream, perform for Nieberding in therapy once a week and spend all my free time, that month of July, with Corey.

I wanted to feel our lovemaking more and I decided that the more sex we had, the safer I was from the frenzy. I had thought that making love would trigger it but instead being with a boy who loved me and whom I loved had seemed to calm me. So I stopped taking my meds. I felt more when Corey was inside of me and I always cried. But it was a good cry, a release.

"Are you okay?" he asked over and over, kissing my face.

"Yes. It feels good to feel," I would tell him. I needed to cry as much as I needed to feel pleasure.

"Well, I guess my music mixes are finally working on you, baby," he said.

Maybe I should tell him, I thought. But I could never bring myself to do it.

I liked to pretend that I was cured; maybe love had cured me.

We stopped going to the woods. I was afraid that Sasha or the boys might find me so we went out into the cornfields instead.

I missed the woods. I longed for them, actually, the

way you want to taste certain delicious foods you're deathly allergic to, or the way you touch someone you love when it has been too long. I dreamed about the woods at night and it felt so real, as if I were running through the darkness with my scary, beautiful brothers, following the scent in the air that would lead us to our prey. I woke with the ache in my hips and teeth and had to touch myself to make sure I hadn't changed. I sniffed my skin for the scent of the forest and felt for leaves in my hair, wondering if I had wandered into the old grove in my sleep and found my way back to bed. But I knew I could only go in my dreams. And besides, I had Corey's body and his sweet words to help me forget.

Corey didn't question the change of location. He just seemed happy to be alone with me. There was an abandoned barn on the outside of town and we made love there as the last light of the day slanted through the broken beams.

On the Fourth of July we climbed all the way up onto the roof and watched the fireworks from the show at the college field cascade down the sky. There were big booms of red, white and blue and explosions of poison green but my favorite ones were the pale white-gold shimmers like something angelic.

I told Corey and he said, "You're my angel."

"I'm so not," I answered.

"My fallen angel, then."

"No doubt."

Sometimes if I'd had an especially hard day I'd be distracted by the faint scent of farm animals in the barn and I felt a weird urge—a frantic stirring that started in my stomach—but then I only kissed Corey harder and forgot my appetite and was satisfied that way. I got home by dark so my mom and dad stayed off my back. Sometimes I took a chance by sneaking out at night through the window, locking my door from the inside behind me. I figured my mom and dad trusted me enough, now that I was in therapy and keeping up an act of following all their rules. I think my dad was ashamed about the time he hit me so he gave me more space than he had before. Maybe Nieberding had had a talk with him. Sometimes on weekends I could get away with staying out later legitimately, if I told them I was with Pace. He always covered for me.

But during that time I shut Pace out, too. I was so dizzy with love for Corey, and fear that it might end, that I might change, that I wasn't there for my best friend. After whatever had happened with the guy, Michael, Pace had kind of shut down on me but I guess I also had pulled away from him a little when our relationship seemed to bother my boyfriend.

We saw each other only a few times, Pace and I. The last time, we went back to the house on Green. He asked me to go with him but I wish I had told him not to go.

"Why are we here?" I asked. "I thought you didn't want to go back."

"It's okay now," he said. His voice was soft, too soft, resigned, but I didn't understand what that meant then.

We sat inside there, just looking around at the shadows, shivering with cold, and he took off his button-down—the kind he always wore with under-shirts—and gave it to me to put on over my tank top. He insisted. He said it looked good on me and when we left he made me keep it. I wore it home even though I was hot by then. I hung it in my closet and forgot about it.

I forgot about the shirt in the same way I had neglected one of the only people who accepted me as I was when maybe I could have helped him.

Full Moon

I had even started avoiding Joe Ranger. But one night crossing the plaza on my way to meet Corey, I saw the rushing shadows of skateboarders—Carl Olaf and his friends. To avoid them, I turned and found myself in front of Joe's prosthetics shop. He was drinking from a can of Red Bull and wiping the sweat off his brow.

"There you are," he growled.

I had trouble looking at him. "Hi, Joey."

"You been avoiding me."

"No, I just see Corey a lot lately. He's leaving for New York soon."

Joe nodded and took something out of his work-shirt pocket. It was a tiny rabbit. He petted it gently with his thumb. I couldn't help smiling when I saw it.

"Who's that?" I asked.

"Stella. She's like a kitten, huh?"

"You do have a way with them," I said.

"I used to have a way with them but one won't come chat anymore." He gave me a knowing look and I avoided his gaze again.

"One," meaning me. But I'd meant animals when I said "them," and Joe knew it, too.

"They get skittish around the full moon," he said. "Know why?"

I shook my head. Didn't really want him to tell me but I knew he wouldn't stop now.

"Predator and prey. They know they're more visible, more in danger. When it wanes they can relax a little."

He was right to use the word *skittish*. That's how I felt. "I have to go meet Corey," I said.

"Yeah. But don't be a stranger." Joe winked.

I nodded and waved to him.

"Watch out for those woods," he called. "Full moon coming."

And it did, as it inevitably does. They say it can make you mad.

Maybe that is what happened with the full moon murderer.

Maybe that is what happened with Pace.

I only know that when I got home at sunset the next day, after making love with Corey in the barn, my mom was on the phone and her face looked pale and tight. She was standing at the sink, holding on to the counter for support and her voice was low. When she saw me her eyes flashed and I knew it was something bad.

"What?" I kept saying it until she got off the phone.

"Pace."

"What about Pace?"

She came toward me and I backed away. "Come sit," she said.

"No! What is it? What happened?"

"Olivia. I need you to breathe."

"Tell me!"

"He passed away," my mom said.

"What? He what?"

I watched myself clawing my fingernails along my arms like they belonged to someone else.

"Liv!" She tried to hold me but I wrenched myself away and she stumbled in her high heels.

"What?" I kept saying over and over. "Passed away? What is that? You mean dead? He's dead?"

"He took his life," she said, and I thought I saw her crossing herself, but very quickly.

I forced my teeth into my lip, trying to break the skin, to taste my own blood. I thought about how little I'd seen him for the last month, how sad he had been about Michael, how I hadn't been there for him. I kept trying to rewind the sequence of events in my mind, go back to when we were talking on the phone and he was telling me about the hottie he met in the house on Green. If I could stop it there, then redo the rest. He had said, "Maybe things are changing for us, Skirt." But he hadn't meant this way. Pace, my brother, my best friend. Playing *Little Earthquakes* for me. Writing Tori lyrics on my blue jeans. Letting me comb his hair, soft and gold as the silk inside a cornstalk. Watching him at football practice pretending to be tough and straight and then we'd go home and sing our favorite songs in my room and paint each other's toenails. I had to take the polish off of him afterward, though, because someone might see in the locker room. Weird the things you think of so you don't see the images in your mind of how he actually did it, took his life. With a rope. Around his neck. With a rope.

I wanted to scream everything at my mother. *You don't know who I am! You don't know who Pace is! Everything is a lie—everything! It's all your fault! It's all your fault!*

But I knew it was just as much my fault. For not calling Pace more. For letting him hurt alone. For not seeing the signs. Maybe even for being born.

I smacked my lips together, saliva accumulating

in the corners or my mouth. My skin itched and my skull and hips ached. I had my period and it felt like blood was pouring out of me, all of my blood, leaving me drained, a lifeless corpse. I backed up, glaring at my mother. I could hear Sasha's voice whispering in my mind.

Kill your mother. Kill her.

"Stop it!" my mom shouted at me. "You're scaring me. Stop hurting yourself."

I looked down and saw streaks of blood on my arms. A salty taste burned on my lips. Soon the hair would grow, my limbs would change, the monster would appear.

I had to flee.

Before I could think anything more I was out the door, heading toward the woods.

News travels fast in small towns and Corey was already on his way to me. I'd left my phone at home so I didn't get his call but as I rounded the bend toward the woods he was there. He had known somehow that this was where I was going. But I couldn't let him see me. I was already changing.

"Liv!" He shouted at me to stop and picked up his pace.

I ran faster, sure I could outrun him. But Corey was pumping his arms and legs, adrenaline bursting through his body, and he caught up just as I dove in among the trees.

I stopped in my tracks and looked over my shoulder. "Leave me alone! Go away from me!" I snarled.

Corey watched me steadily, concerned but not afraid, even though I knew my eyes must have looked like the eyes of a demon. My teeth were cutting my gums. Drool spilled from the corner of my lip. My ears twitched, turning this way and that, listening for signs of danger. The sounds and smells were starting to overwhelm me, banging in my ears, burning my nostrils. My skull hurt, lengthening as it filled with too much sensation. I lowered my head to the ground.

I tugged off my shirt and then struggled out of my jeans. Night was coming on fast and I could feel the pull of the moon rising slowly above the forest.

"Liv," Corey said softly.

"Pace! Oh my God, Pace."

"I know, baby." He reached out his hand.

"And I'm changing, I'm going to . . . You can't see me like this."

"Liv." His voice reminded me of the one he used with the animals at the vet's. "Don't be scared. I know what you are."

I couldn't speak anymore. I just looked up at him and my eyes felt like they were on fire in the sockets. I cocked my head, trying to ask him the question. *How do you know?*

"I chased after you that night last month when we fought." It was as if he'd read my thoughts.

I glared at him.

"I'm sorry. I wanted to see if you trusted me enough to tell me yourself. And I saw that you didn't."

My mind raced back over the events of that night. *You mean you saw me change?*

He nodded.

He had seen me. And he was here now.

"I saw you change and I saw you change back. I followed you again to make sure you got home safely. You were naked. I was worried about you. But I didn't want to let you know I was there."

This was Corey. The Corey I had known for years. Corey who would never judge me or leave me, even if I changed into a monster in front of his eyes. Even if I ran naked through the woods and lay on the ground eating freshly killed meat. It made no sense and yet it made perfect sense to me because I knew him.

But I had not trusted him.

And now I had to run. My limbs were changing. They refused to stay still. Pain shot through me; the only relief would be to move.

Go home, leave me.

He didn't listen. As I ran he followed, deeper

into the woods. I heard him struggling to keep up—
the ragged sound of his breath—and sometimes he
would gasp out my name. We came to a glade and the
moon shone brightly through the trees on my monster
body.

I stopped to look up at the round white light in the
sky. Corey slumped beside me, his sides heaving.

"Since when you outpace me like that?" he gasped.

Outpace.

We both stared at each other as the shock returned.
Corey turned his head away and to the side, bit his lip
trying to keep back the tears. My heart was pounding pain through my veins. I looked up at the sky and
howled my grief to the moon.

When I could make no more sounds I looked around
me. A circle of golden eyes watched us from the darkness. Fourteen golden eyes. My brothers.

I got to my feet. The transformation was complete
now and I wasn't weak from it anymore. The ache and
pain had turned to strength, a feeling of great power.

I could have run all night with my pack. The moment had come.

But then I looked at Corey, who had moved so that he stood behind me. He had followed me here. He had made love to me for a month, even knowing what I was and that I would not tell him the truth about it. Corey was my family now, the only one I had. Pace was gone, my parents would never know me and the seven wolves watching in the darkness wanted something I could never give them. I thought about the deaths in the woods and wondered who was responsible, what these creatures could do to a boy in the woods at night, no matter how brave or compassionate he was. All this went through my mind and I turned slowly in a circle, making eye contact with each brother. Amorus. Gregory. Frederick. Marcos. Felix. Sebastian. Victor.

Leave us! He is mine.

Victor, the largest wolf, snarled, his eyes glowing like golden mirrors in the darkness as he looked at Corey.

For now. There was a sneer in the wolf voice.

I didn't understand what he meant but I knew he was not done with me yet. And I also knew I had won, at least this time. He lowered his head in submission, then turned and slunk into the woods. The others followed him.

I dropped to the ground, wriggled forward on my belly and rested my chin on Corey's leg.

"Who the hell were they?" he said.

I could smell his flesh through his clothes and I wanted to taste him. I *could* almost taste him—the sweet, salty sensation a memory on my lips. But I had not forgotten my prayer.

May the winds of calm . . .

Pace was dead, I had changed, but this was Corey, the one I loved. And somewhere inside, beneath the teeth sharp enough to pulverize bone, the muscles that could take down an elk, the fur rough enough to protect from cold and wet, somewhere beneath it all I was still me.

I'm sorry, Corey. I love you.

He nodded as if he'd heard me, then stroked my head until that full moon fell and only redemptive dawn lit the sky.

Death

By morning I had changed back again. We didn't speak about any of what had happened—even Pace; it was too much. Corey found my clothes near the entrance to the woods. He walked me to the stream, sat me down in the shallow water, bathed me, dried me off with his sweatshirt and dressed me. Everything hurt and my stomach was growling with hunger. It was all I could think about, or all I wanted to think about, wiping out any thoughts or feelings of grief. I limped home on Corey's arm and he kissed me good-bye at my door. The day was already growing hot and the sun shot harsh rays into my eyes as we emerged from the trees.

Part of me wished my dad had hit me again to take my mind off everything. But my parents seemed to have forgiven me for running because of what had happened to Pace. They were in the kitchen drinking coffee and for once the TV wasn't on. Gramp slept sitting up on the couch. My dad didn't say anything. My mom asked me what I needed and I pointed to the refrigerator. Then I walked over to the freezer and took out a slab of red meat marbled with streaks of white.

They both stared at me. "You want a steak?" my mom said.

I nodded. I didn't want to hear a lecture about anemia right then but I'd have done anything for some rare meat.

"You must be anemic. You look pale. I told you. Let me cook you up something. Go upstairs and get in bed. I'll bring it. I told you young people shouldn't be vegetarians!"

She went on like that as I climbed up the stairs, threw my clothes on the floor and got in bed. The sheets felt cool and soft against my skin. My mom was obsessed with thread count and for once I was grateful. I smelled the meat cooking in a pan on the stove. My nostrils tingled with sensation and my mouth watered; my stomach growled so loudly it sounded as if there were an animal in the room. When my mom finally came with the steak I sat up and devoured it in a few bites. My teeth still felt sharper than usual and my tongue longer, my mouth bigger. I wiped my greasy lips with the back of my hand and gave my mother the tray. Then I lay back down, closed my eyes and slept.

When I woke it was the next evening. I felt nauseous and confused. For a moment I lay there in a fog, trying to think of what it was I didn't want to remember.

Yes, Pace. That was it. No. Yes. What?

Pace was dead.

My best friend. The only one I trusted besides Corey. And dead because he hated himself. Because he didn't accept himself. That was partly why we had been friends. Because we both felt this same way. And it had won, the self-hatred. It had killed him.

I curled up in a ball and shut my eyes but I couldn't sleep again.

I would have slept straight through if I could have; slept through forever. Corey kept calling until I answered.

"Come outside with me," he said. "Baby, come outside and breathe."

But I couldn't get out of bed. Not even for Corey. And he couldn't come to me because of my parents. I was too weary even to care about that. So I stayed in bed for two days—not able to read, completely unable to write in my diary—until Pace's funeral and then I put on black jeans and a black Sex Pistols T-shirt turned inside out under Pace's cotton button-down and went to the cemetery with my mom, my dad and Gramp.

We stood on the sloping hillside full of the graves of men who had died in the steel mill—crushed by steel, burned by molten steel—men and women who had died of old age, cancer, heart attacks and grief, children who had died of illness and accidents, babies who had died at birth. They all lay beneath our feet, under their carved gray granite headstones and giant crosses that shadowed the lawn, and Pace would be there, too. But it was impossible that Pace could be there with the dead. I could still see his face and hear the sound of his voice. His scent of goat's milk soap and citrusy aftershave was still on the shirt he had let me wear home. I could still feel his lips.

Once Pace and I had kissed. Just once. I think we were trying to prove something to ourselves—maybe that we weren't the things we feared.

We were dancing to old David Bowie in my room. *"We can be heroes, just for one day."* Pace was so much taller than me; I just came to the middle of his chest. One of his big hands held mine, and the other rested on the small of my back. He turned me around gracefully but with force and I tossed my hair. It was right after the first frenzy and more than anything I just wanted to be a regular girl. Pace must have wanted, in that moment, to be a "normal" boy. He touched his lips to mine. It was awkward and sweet and he tasted of peppermint toothpaste. Then he pulled away and we both broke into giggles. We laughed so hard we fell to the ground.

We were what we were. And in that moment, because we had each other, it was okay.

But Pace hadn't felt okay, even though there was nothing wrong with what he was. Pace wasn't a monster like me. He was just a boy who loved boys.

I watched the men digging the grave and thought that I wanted to go down there with Pace, down where it was dark and quiet and safe. Where I couldn't hurt anyone ever again. Tears poured down my face and slid saltily into my mouth. I saw Pace's parents clinging to each other like stunned children. They were rich, tall, blond and good-looking. They had once had a handsome, athletic son who they had never really known at all. Carolyn Carter, the waitress at the café where Pace worked, was with them. She glared at me and I hung my head.

I looked around for a boy about my age, a cute boy I didn't recognize, just in case this mysterious Michael had heard what had happened and found his way there. But there were very few young men at all.

After the ceremony I went over to Pace's parents and hugged them, trying not to look at Carolyn. They felt almost boneless with grief. Their eyes were blank. I didn't have words to say but I tried anyway.

"I'm so sorry."

"Thank you."

The words you are supposed to say when what you mean is so much more. You feel denial and empathy and anger and blame and fear and sorrow and all you can say are words. In some ways animals have it better, I thought.

I looked up. Corey stood across the plot from me, watching with his greenish brown eyes. The boy I loved. He knew what I was and he hadn't run away. I saw my mother watching as Corey hugged me lightly and kissed my cheek. I wanted to turn and kiss him on the mouth but I was afraid. Not of what she would do but of what would happen if she made me angry. So I pulled away from him quickly.

"I want to show you something," he said.

Next to Pace's grave was an old gravestone with a huge sad-eyed angel bending over it like a willow tree. Carved into the stone were the words: MICHAEL FAIRBORN, JULY 10, 1896—SEPTEMBER 2, 1913.

"Michael?" I said.

"Wasn't there something about a guy who hung himself in the house on Green Street?" Corey asked me.

Hung himself? Like what Pace had done. With a rope in his closet. I shuddered. "The Fairborn House. *Michael* Fairborn."

Corey and I exchanged a look. Michael. Like Pace's

Michael? I had never seen this Michael guy. He had never showed up at the funeral. He was like an apparition. The names could have been a coincidence but I wasn't so sure. Maybe Pace imagined Michael or maybe there was more to it. Nothing made sense in the normal way anymore.

I shivered, remembering the icy house. Corey moved closer to me so I could feel the hairs on my arm brush against his smooth skin. I wasn't embarrassed by them now. In the light of what had happened, small things like that meant nothing.

I wanted to tell Pace what I was thinking. *I don't understand what happened with Michael. But whatever it was I wish I could have helped you. I let you down. I turned away from you. Without your love and acceptance, without Corey, I could have been where you are now. Love is the only thing we have to save us.*

"What do you think that means?" Corey asked. "That they had the same name. That Pace did it the way he did."

I wished Pace was there so I could ask him. No matter what he said, I wouldn't have judged it; I would have just listened.

"But you know about things I don't understand, baby." Corey took my chin in his hand and lifted my face gently so our eyes met. "Like what happened with those wolves the other night."

"I'll tell you everything I know," I said and the tears came with it and he reached out and took my hand even though people might have seen us. *Fuck it, I thought. Pace is dead and I'm going to worry if my mom sees this? I didn't pull away.*

I looked across the cemetery lawn and saw Joe Ranger standing by himself with his hands in his pockets, watching me. Even from that far away I could see his jaw working, chewing tobacco like he was devouring a piece of raw meat.

Perhaps my friend Pace, in love with a ghost, had lost his mind. But who was to say that I had not?

August Kill

We only had a few more weeks before the end of the summer; that was when Corey would be going away from me. Now that Pace was gone I clung to my boyfriend more than ever. Without him, with everything that had happened, I was afraid it would be so easy for me to move in the direction Pace had gone.

I went back to work and Corey started picking me up in the evening instead of meeting me at the barn. We walked together through town, not caring if anyone saw us. Part of me wanted the news to get back to my mom so I could finally tell her the truth.

Sometimes in the heady heat of late summer everything seemed like a dream—Sasha, the brothers, the haunted house, the thing that had happened to Pace. I wanted to believe that the wolf woman was a dream, too. I didn't want that to be real. All I had to do, I told myself, was to keep away from the strange people who lived in the forest.

But I knew it really wasn't as simple as that, not at all. Three things had to be present to activate the curse—a full moon, my menstrual blood and an outburst of my rage. At least that was how it had been every time and the moon, my cycle and my anger were not as easy to avoid as a forest.

I was still seeing Nieberding to appease my parents but he was starting to really make my nerves crawl. After Pace's death he watched me more carefully and kept asking how Pace being gone made me feel. I didn't want to go through the emotions again because I was afraid I'd frenzy, so I tried to change the subject. The sessions were grueling and I left feeling weak from the discipline. Sometimes, afterward, I'd notice how long and jagged my fingernails suddenly looked. I had to be careful when I kissed Corey because my teeth felt sharper. And the hair kept growing on my body.

There was a brutal, desperate feeling in the air that summer, like when you smell a fire, a big fire, but you don't know where it's coming from. The town lay under a stupor. The heat made it hard to move or breathe and all around me I sensed danger. But most of all I sensed it from inside myself.

Now that Corey was picking me up after work I stopped walking past Joe Ranger's. I thought of how he'd watched me in the cemetery and the way he'd talked about the full moon coming. I wasn't sure who or what Joe was and I didn't know if I trusted him anymore. He had taken me to Sasha and seemed to be her friend. Maybe he wanted me to kill my mother, too. So I avoided Joe Ranger until I had no other choice except to seek him out and ask him for his help.

It was late at night, after I'd left Corey. I woke from a nightmare of being in the prosthetics shop. Real severed limbs hung from the walls. The flesh was mottled like blue cheese or dripping with blood like raw meat in a butcher's shop. When I opened my eyes I was so disoriented that the figure standing at my bedside seemed part of the nightmare.

But he was real.

He was a tall, dark-haired young man with luminous, yellow eyes and red roses—so dark they almost looked black—in his arms.

Victor.

"Don't be afraid," he said. His voice was deep and soft and his eyes were fixed on mine. I could feel him willing me not to scream and it worked. Besides, the last thing I wanted was for my father to come. I just stared back at Victor. My thighs were sweating into the sheet.

"I won't hurt you, Olivia."

"Get the hell out!" I hissed when I could finally talk.

"I just need to talk to you for a little while. Is that all right? May I speak with you? May I sit?"

He gestured to a chair by my bed but I didn't answer him.

"I brought you roses. May I leave them here?" He laid the roses at the foot of my bed. They had a strong scent that made my head spin the way it did when I frenzied. It was as if I had two hundred million smelling cells inside my nose.

"I don't think my boyfriend will be okay with that," I said. "You know him. The one you threatened."

Victor ignored me. "We have been respectful."

He bowed his head and dropped to his knees.

"Get up!" I growled. "My dad will come."

Victor's eyes flicked up at me. "I'm not afraid of

your father." There was a sneer in his voice.

"I'm not going to go anywhere with you."

He moved closer to me and in spite of how he and his brothers had circled me and Corey in the woods I felt a desire to reach out and touch the top of his head. His hair looked thick, coarse but lush. Saliva filled my mouth and my heart was pounding. There would be a full moon soon. There always was eventually. I wondered if the more times I desired to change, the more easily I would change when the circumstances were right.

"Your mother is downstairs, asleep," Victor said softly. "But she wears a silver cross on her breast day and night. She is safe from me. She is safe from everyone."

But not from me, I thought. That was what Victor was thinking; I knew it. I was the one who could slip into my mother's room, when the moon was not full and I did not bleed, remove the silver from her neck, hide it and, later, before she found it, take her life.

"Olivia, I am here for something else."

I shivered at the intensity of his words that came from deep in his throat. I had to admit his face was beautiful in the moonlight—broad, high cheekbones, a cleft in his chin, wide-set eyes that tilted up slightly at the outer corners under heavy arched brows.

"I never met any females who were like me," he went on. "So I was excited to meet you. We all were. We overheard our mother talk about you. We used to come to town once a year looking when it became almost unbearable to be alone. But you aren't just important because of that." He lowered his head again. His eyelashes made spiky shadows on his cheeks. "I am capable of many things. . . ." His pause was ominous. "You could redeem me."

Redeem him? What did that mean? It frightened me but it also intrigued me—it made me feel a certain sense of power, but power that was dependent on his attention to, and need for, me.

In spite of myself I felt something I couldn't name

pump through my veins. What would it be like to touch a young man like this? A man who deeply understood what I was. Who was what I was.

The unnamed thing was desire.

No, Liv, stop.

"I saw you with the *boy*," Victor said, curling the last word with his tongue. "I've seen you with him for years. I can tell he loves you. Now. But he is leaving for the city while you stay here."

"How do you know that?" I had to force myself to keep from screaming for my parents. But I knew that would only make this all worse.

Victor didn't answer the question. "*I'm* not going anywhere," was all he said.

"Yes, you are! Get out of here!" I stumbled from the bed, not caring that he saw me in my underwear, the soft layer of red hair sprouting all over my body. The roses scattered on the floor as I pulled the blanket off and wrapped it around me.

Victor slunk toward the window, still gazing up at

me with his gold eyes.

"I can teach you things," he said. "Things you need to know to survive with this curse you have. The boy can teach you nothing. He will never be enough for you. Come to me before you have no other choice."

And then he was on the ledge. I watched him leap down to the garden below, the way no boy could leap. He turned to look up at me one last time before he vanished into the night.

I could smell the perfume of roses like beautiful poison.

After Victor's visit I knew I had to see Joe Ranger. He had knowledge I needed. I couldn't go looking for Sasha, Victor or the others—even after the visit I was still trying to pretend they weren't real, it hadn't happened—but Joe was real, and he wasn't hidden away in the woods. And maybe he had some answers.

So one night, when Corey had to stay late at work, I went back to the shop.

It looked closed—door locked, sign out—but I knocked and waited. After a long time I heard footsteps and he came to the front of the shop. The light was dim but I could see Joe's green eyes very well.

"Livia, what's shakin'?"

"Me," I said. "Most of the time."

"Come on in, girl."

The shop had a strange musty, metallic smell. I followed Joe into the back room. I'd never been there before. There were two old-fashioned upholstered armchairs and a small table. Cooper slept on the floor next to the fan. Joe motioned for me to sit down and he gave me a bottle of water.

We were silent for a while, studying each other. "What's on your mind?"

"I had a weird dream about the shop," I said.

"Yeah?" He scowled a little. "Do tell."

"There were real limbs hanging everywhere."

Joe bared his teeth for a quick second, then his face went back to normal. "Not a pretty sight."

"And then Victor came to visit me." I hadn't expected to tell him that. Saying Victor's name out loud to someone else made it all more real. Or maybe it just made me seem crazier to myself.

"Came to your house, did he?" Joe shook his head. "Boy's getting bold. What did he want? I told him to lay off."

"I think you know."

Joe shook his head again. "I don't know nothing for sure anymore."

It seemed pointless to pretend after everything that had happened. "But you're one."

He had his head down, while he stroked Cooper's exposed belly, but his eyes shot up at me. The pupils were pricks of dark in the bright green irises.

"One what?"

"You know what I'm talking about."

"This ain't about what I am or am not," he said.

Joe stood up, all six-foot-two of him rising above me. He leaned back against the wall and looked at me.

I had never thought to really be afraid of him before in spite of my parents' warnings. The air in the room felt stifling and hot. Corey wouldn't know where I had gone. . . .

"Then tell me about what I am. I don't know how to control this thing and there's no one I can ask."

"There's nothing I can teach you," Joe said. "You need to learn it for yourself."

"But I think you know how to control it. You don't live in fear, away from everyone."

"I told you, this ain't about the way I roll." Joe cocked a bushy eyebrow at me.

"Sasha said it was connected to rage."

He grinned so his big teeth showed. "What do you think?"

"It was rage for me, but only when I had my . . . when I'm on my cycle and the moon's full." I felt my cheeks turning red. "I could control it before—the anger. But not in the last two months."

"I've been working with rage my whole life. You

don't just learn how to manage by having some elder statesman, no matter how wise"—he cleared his throat, winked and patted his chest—"tell you what to do. You have to work it out by yourself."

But you know, I wanted to shout. *You know!*

I looked at him standing against the wall. "How did you become one?" I asked him.

There was something almost vicious about his grin now. "You don't stop, do you?"

"Were you cursed, like me? Or did you change some other way?"

"Time to leave now," Joe said.

Then I remembered how Sasha and Joe had looked at each other at the cabin door. "Does it have something to do with Sasha? Can we change people who aren't born like us? Did she . . ."

Joe shook his head, long and slow. "I said time to leave."

I didn't protest. When I looked into his eyes I knew there wasn't any more I could say to change his mind.

* ✿ *

I didn't sleep at all that night, just lay awake thinking. The shadows on the wall grew teeth and snarled
at me. The next night when I knew Joe Ranger would
be leading his AA meeting at the café where Pace used
to work I told Corey I had some things to do for my
mom and went back to the shop. I walked around the
back and jiggled the door. It was locked, of course. But
I saw a small window up at the top. I could climb up
there—I was a good climber. And I could fit through.
No one was around to see.

When I lowered myself into the tiny bathroom
with the cracked green tile I was suddenly sick with
fear. What if he came back? I had to kneel on the floor
with my head down for a moment to calm myself. Fireworks were shooting through my brain and dropping
corrosive sparks down my throat into my stomach.
May the great mother protect me. Finally I was able to crawl
into the little bedroom next to the bath. It was very
dark with a large bed covered in a red quilt. Not much

else of interest. I got up and walked into the room with the two chairs—not much there either. There was also a tiny kitchen with a mini refrigerator and a microwave. Nothing. I went back into the bedroom and opened some dresser drawers—just T-shirts, jeans, underwear and socks. I pawed through a stack of papers on a bureau. A few bills. Closet? Joe's denim and leather jackets and a few button-down shirts, his boots. I got down on my hands and knees and looked under the bed. There was an old leather-bound trunk. I pulled it out and opened it.

They were photos and newspaper clippings mostly. I lifted them out and spread them on the floor. I found a picture of Joe as a kid with a giant parrot perched on his shoulder. Another of him with a big dog, a fishing pole in his hand. Some more black and whites of what must have been family members. And then I found a photo of a woman wearing a man's fedora hat, peeking up from under the brim. She was topless and her lips were curved in a soft smile. It was Sasha.

Under that were some newspaper clippings that read:

"Full Moon Killer Strikes Again."

"Full Moon Murders."

"Serial Animal? Who Will Be Next?"

They were from the last four years, the period of time since my mother had killed the wolf. Had Sasha met Joe then, bitten him? Had he changed and was he now the murderer? Is that how it worked, could you bite someone and make them become like you? And what did Joe want with me? What was I to him? And what came next?

There was another picture under the newspaper clippings.

It was a picture of me.

I was about three years old, wearing a bathing suit with ruffles. My skin looked very light in the bright sun. I was playing in the fountain in the town square, laughing as the water spurted out at me from the mouths of demons.

I looked back at the newspaper articles. It struck me then, for the first time. How had I not noticed it before? Carl Olaf's dad, Reed, just a week after Carl Olaf laughed at me. My one supposed girlfriend Sadie Nelson's father, Loudon. Hair-tying Sherry Lee's father, Bob. Rude Dale Tamblin's father, Dan. They were all hunters, yes, out in the woods on the night of a full moon. But that wasn't uncommon in this town—people hunted by the bright moonlight. Almost everyone in this town hunted. But not almost everyone in this town had a child or spouse who had insulted or hurt me in some way. Not almost everyone in town had a child who had occupied space in my diary, the diary that had been open one morning when I was sure I had closed it the night before.

I heard a noise and jumped, covering my mouth with my hand as waves of cold air rippled through me. It was only Joe's black cat. It hissed at me and I backed toward the bathroom.

As I slid through the window and jumped down

into the night I saw a truck pull up from the road into the drive. I'd been at Joe's longer than I'd thought. The headlights caught me for a moment before I got away.

Joe Ranger had seen me. And I understood him even less now than before. And I was more afraid of him.

The next day at breakfast I asked my father. I tried to sound casual. It helped that the news was on because I could pretend that it had reminded me about the killings.

"Did you ever find out more about those hunters that died in the woods?" I asked him as I nonchalantly chewed my cornflakes.

He took a sip of coffee and looked at me. It almost seemed painful for him to look directly at me, especially lately. "You mean the full moon murders?"

I nodded.

My mom bustled around pouring more coffee.

"Can we not talk shop here? It's disturbing."

"I never ask Dad about his work," I said.

She switched the channel to *America's Next Top Model* reruns. She knew each episode almost by heart.

"She looks exactly like a boy. She needs to stop lifting weights and start eating something like Lisa told her. You'd think they put another transgendered one on."

"Now that's disgusting talk at the table," my father said.

"But do you have any clues? I mean do you think it could happen again?"

He shrugged. "It could always happen again. Everything could always happen again. Why do you think I don't want you near those woods? It's not for shits and giggles."

I had to hide the shudder that went through my body. I had never really been afraid of the full moon murderer before. But I thought of Joe Ranger's strange green eyes watching me illuminated in his headlights.

I wasn't so sure that I was safe from anything anymore. At the same time I didn't want to bring up his name. As much as he scared me, part of me still wanted to protect him until I was sure.

"So no clues?" I said as I stared at the TV, where a beautiful girl in black eyeliner was posing with her hand on her ass.

"I can't discuss it," my dad said. "Since when are you interested?"

I shrugged. My mom said, "She's just trying to make conversation with you, Jeff. She's reaching out. You could try to indulge her."

I got up. "No, it's okay," I said.

"I need a manicure today." My mom had sat down and was examining her cuticles. "Do you want to come after work?"

I looked at my ragged fingernails. "No thanks," I said.

"We're going out of town next weekend," she told me. "You'll have the house to yourself. Maybe you could invite some girlfriends over. You need people."

Yeah, right. Like I had girlfriends.

"You need to start making friends now, new friends."

"Okay," I said. And I left the room.

When I think back on that time I remember my hand throbbing a warning. But maybe I just imagine it now.

My mom had distracted me but I wasn't done talking to my dad about the full moon murders. So the next afternoon I decided to stop by the police station. I rode my bike there, along the deserted pathways of the campus, among the peeling-barked sycamore trees that hung heavy and yellow-green with heat. The brick buildings of the college always seemed weird in the summer, just much too quiet. I tried to imagine going to school there in the fall but it made me feel like I couldn't breathe right. I was afraid it would be high school all over again—the isolation, the embarrass-ment—while Corey escaped to a city that was never quiet or completely dark and where monsters like me roamed freely and unnoticed in the streets.

I passed Ravenwood Hall at the edge of campus, a dark gray stone Victorian building with columns in front. The dorm was overgrown with vines and stood behind a wrought-iron gate. This was another report-edly haunted place in our town. It had originally been a mental asylum. There were secret underground pas-sages where the janitor had found used straitjackets, chains and old hypodermic needles after the build-ing had been converted into a dorm. In the fifties a male student had come home late from a dance, heard noises in the hallway and gone out to investigate, leav-ing all his personal belongings in his room and his bed neatly made. He was never seen or heard from again. There were rumors of satanic cults, sexual tor-ture, murder and supernatural events. Students who lived in the dorm talked about unexplained voices in the hallways and strange lights hovering in the trees around the building. A local woman claimed that many years after, a man matching the student's description came to her door one snowy night asking for directions. He was not dressed for the weather, seemed disoriented and had blood on his forehead. When she asked him in and offered to help him, he hurried away into the night.

Corey and Pace and I had gone to explore this building, too. Pace had always said he thought the guy was gay and that he killed himself out of shame or was attacked because of his sexual orientation.

"Why do you think that?" I had asked him.

He had shrugged. "In this town gays are the monsters."

I rode faster past that building, choking back the tears that had suddenly welled up in my throat.

The truth was that the town might have been dangerous for gay people—it had been for my Pace, because if he had felt accepted, maybe he wouldn't have taken his life—and it might be dangerous for monsters like me, but the woods were dangerous for hunters, and the fathers of the kids that had been cruel to me in school.

I got to the police station, left my bike unchained by the stairs and ran up the marble front steps. Jake Cunningham, the deputy at the desk motioned me toward my dad's office. I rarely visited him here. He was sitting behind his desk on the phone. He scowled a little when he saw me.

"Is everything okay?" he asked when he'd hung up.

"Yes, I just needed to talk to you."

I sat down and he waited for me to go on. When I saw him like this, at work, trying to take care of people, serious and sober, it was hard to imagine him hitting me in the face.

"I was just wondering about that thing we were talking about."

"Olivia, I'm working."

"I know. I've just been kind of freaked out."

He leaned back in his chair and patted his belly. He'd gained a little weight lately but you could still see the athlete in his body. "These killings have been going on for years. Why the interest now?"

I wished I hadn't come; he looked like he was getting suspicious.

"I guess I've been more nervous about everything since what happened with . . . Pace."

"That's something to talk to your doctor about, isn't it?" he said. His voice was kinder than usual. Behind him was a picture of our family. My mom looked beautiful, like a mom in an advertisement, and my dad had his arm firmly around her. I looked okay, almost normal. It had been taken when I was twelve and he'd never replaced it with a newer one.

"No, it's all right." I stood up.

"Olivia, is there something you're not telling me?" he asked. "About the murders? Something someone told you? Anything at all?"

"I just can't handle another disaster," I said. "I miss Pace."

He nodded and scowled some more. "I know."

"I have to go." I stopped at the door and turned back to him. "That student, that guy who disappeared in the fifties, do you think they'll ever find out what happened to him?"

"It's still an open case. Endangered missing. He didn't just not show up. There was all kinds of suspicious stuff around it. Why?"

"It's just weird. Another weird thing about this town."

My dad shook his head and stared at the top of his desk. "Liv, think about what I asked you. It's important that you tell me if there's something you remember."

I was silent.

"I have work to do," he said.

So I left.

The Silver Hand

My mother and father were taking Gramp to view a nursing home they thought he might like when his health "deteriorated" as my mom put it. It was a little far away but was supposed to be the best in the state. I could tell Gramp didn't want to go but when I asked him about it he shrugged.

"I'll finally have some peace and quiet." He winked at me. "How many TVs can one family own; will you tell me that, Olivia?"

"I'll come visit you."

"No, you won't. Those places stink like sewage.

But I'll come see you on holidays and tell you Ellie stories."

"Tell me one now."

We were sitting on white wicker chairs on the sun-porch that looked out at the garden. I'd always liked this room best. It felt like you were outside. I would rather have slept here than in my room and sometimes when I was a little girl I'd sneak down and sleep on the swinging bench and listen to the cicadas.

Gramp tapped his fingers on the glass tabletop. "She was perfect. And I didn't deserve her."

"I'm sure you did."

"Then you'd sure be wrong. I did some bad things in my life, Olivia. Things your mother has never forgiven me for. And she's right. But I've had to learn to forgive myself so I could go on without wreaking more havoc. And if you can forgive yourself, you can forgive others. That's the only way you can, I think."

I thought I understood what he meant. Every time the moon was full and I bled I had to forgive myself on some level for the thoughts I'd had about my mother when I was thirteen or I would have only felt more rage and been more dangerous to everyone.

When my family left I invited Corey to come stay. We took over the whole house. We lit tall green candles everywhere in the crystal holders and played music as loud as we could. Corey had found this Meat Loaf song from the seventies that started with dialogue about a wolf coming to the door with red roses. *"On a hot summer's night would you offer your throat to the wolf with the red roses?"* It freaked me out because it reminded me of Victor so I made Corey skip to the next song. We ordered takeout Chinese—steamed dumplings, mushu vegetable, stir-fried broccoli—with my mom's credit card and ate in bed out of the white paper cartons watching the Lord of the Rings movies. Plum sauce on our lips when we kissed. We talked about what our life would be like someday when I could move to New York and we'd get a tiny apartment with a claw-foot tub in the kitchen and one raw brick wall and Corey would be a vet and I would be a psychologist. We'd run in Central Park every day and go to the museums and galleries and clubs to hear all the new bands. We'd sample different cheap ethnic cuisine every night. We'd have a very small wardrobe of mostly black clothes that we shared and all our dishes would be mismatched from the Salvation Army. Maybe we'd have a baby. We even joked about the fact that it might be a little pup.

"We'll call him Wolfgang," Corey teased. "Wolf for short. It's a great name. Or Faolon. Little Wolf in Gaelic. I've been researching."

Nothing scared me when I imagined a future like that with Corey. It didn't seem as if there would be any danger anymore, as long as we were together and away from this town. We even forgot, for a moment, that night—or at least we pretended to forget—that our friend Pace would never come visit us in Manhattan the way he had said he would when we had shared our fantasy with him.

On the evening of the full moon we'd been drinking red wine from my dad's liquor cabinet and we lost track of time. Corey should have left before sundown, just to be safe, but instead we were lying on the living room carpet eating chocolate-covered espresso beans with our wine and making out. The first *Underworld* was playing on the big-screen TV. I was half dressed, wearing just underpants and a tank top and Corey only had on his plaid shorts. My head was resting on his smooth chest and my eyes were closed. The air-conditioning was blasting cool over our hot bodies. Kate Beckinsale was running through a Gothic city in her sleek black cat suit.

The door opened and my parents and Gramp came in.

I pushed Corey behind me as if I could hide him with my body and stared at my mother.

My father just turned and walked back outside, swearing. "What the hell. I'm sick of this bullshit!

I'm going out with Jake."

My grandfather went to sit in his chair and put on the TV.

My mother stood her ground. She pushed her glasses up on her nose, crossed her arms over her chest and looked at Corey and me.

"Company?" she said.

"I didn't know you were coming home now."

"Well, yes, it is our house. I didn't know you'd be busy."

Corey grabbed his shirt and slipped it over his head. "Sorry, Mrs. Thorne." He stood up and held out his hand. "I'm Corey Steele. I've gone to school with Liv since first grade."

My mother shook his hand lightly. "First grade? Wow. She didn't tell me about you."

Corey and I exchanged a look. My mom smiled brightly at him, then turned to me. "Are you okay, Olivia?"

She had been asking me if I was all right constantly

since Pace's death. This time there was more to it.

"I'm fine." I put on my cutoffs and grabbed Corey's hand. "I'm going out."

My mother stopped me. "Wait a second. I want to talk to you first."

I looked at Corey and my expression must have been desperate because he nodded as if to say, *It's all right.*

"I'll call you later," he told me.

My mother followed me upstairs and into my room. I sat on my bed and glared at her. "What?"

"I didn't know you were seeing someone so soon."

"So?" I took a few deep breaths. There was no reason I should let myself get out of control. I couldn't let her get to me that easily.

"I know this thing with Pace has been hard for you. It isn't easy to lose a boyfriend like that."

I turned away. *He wasn't my boyfriend, Mom.*

"But that isn't a reason to act out like this."

I circled around to face her. Saliva seemed to boil

over in my mouth. My skin itched and my teeth and nail beds ached.

"Mother," I said, as quietly as I could, "Corey is my boyfriend. Not Pace. Pace was my friend, but not my boyfriend. He just pretended to help me out because I was afraid of what you would say. I loved Pace in a different way and he died pretending he was something he wasn't. And I'm sick of being afraid."

"Liv . . ."

"Give me one reason why it is a problem that I am seeing Corey? One reason! Say it!"

She cleared her throat and pushed her glasses back up on her nose. "You don't even know . . ."

"I know him better than I know you and Dad. I know him better than I know myself!"

"You should have told me," my mother said, straightening out her blouse.

"Why? What would you have said? You would have been happy about it?"

She stood up. "I don't think you understand. There's

nothing wrong with mixed race couples per se but it can cause you a lot of problems down the road."

Pain shot through my hips. I could feel blood coming out of my body. My hands shook.

"Think of the children—I mean that alone . . ."

I did think of the children. They had cocoa skin and green eyes. They had soft, loose curls and Corey's smile. The problem wasn't Corey. The problem was if they were born creatures like me.

"Get out of my room!" I yelled. "Just get the hell out!" It wasn't only about my anger now; it was about protecting her. The moon was rising. I could feel it in my marrow.

"We'll talk this over with Dr. N.," she said. She went to the door, stopped and looked back at me. "I don't think you're fully aware of the consequences of your actions and that's part of what becoming an adult means. If you and this boy are having sexual relations it can get especially complicated considering the circumstances."

A growl came up from my belly and I tried to stifle it. She went away and I lunged toward the window. If I leaped now and ran fast I might be able to get to the woods in time to save her from me.

But I didn't make it.

The woods. Have to get to the woods. The white moon. Pulling, pulling. I have to run but I can't run. The pain of change shoots through my limbs. I press my face into the earth, breathing the scents, intoxicated.

At last the beast raises her muzzle and looks around, confused. Where are the woods?

But the beast is in a garden full of orange lilies and lacy green trees with softly peeling bark.

"There's a wolf in the garden," my grandfather says from his chair.

A woman steps out the back door. She wears pink lipstick and her hair is perfect. She looks at the beast, startled, and cocks the gun on her shoulder. On her breasts, under her clothes, lies the silver cross. The beast can't see it but she can feel it, burning her own skin, branding her.

The beast wants to leap for the woman's throat but I won't let her because I am still here, too.

As I whirl to run for the woods, the woman raises her gun, aims and hesitates for just a moment.

"Liv?" she cries. Her voice sounds confused. I stop and look at her but she is looking toward the house, up toward the window of my room. She half looks back at me and then she shoots.

My mother is usually a good shot, precise as hell. But anyone can be distracted. And the pain blasts through my paw, shattering fur and muscle, blood and bone.

I dive into the underbrush, limping on three legs, on fire with pain. The other pain, the changing pain, is nothing compared to this.

And that is all I know.

✿ ✿ ✿

I heard beeping sounds and felt the bright light through my eyelids. The air cool and sterile but I could smell death down the corridor. I tried to move but my body was trapped. And somewhere far away and softened by narcotics there was a horrific pain, or the memory of pain.

This was what I felt when I woke finally in the hospital. I opened my eyes, a light flickering attempt that finally succeeded. Corey was at my side.

"Liv!" He stood up and moved closer. "Mom!" He was yelling now. "She's awake."

His face was drawn, dark shadows under his eyes. He pressed his cheek against mine and his skin was cold.

I tried to talk. My lips were chapped and my throat felt closed. I wanted to ask what had happened. Where was my mother? But I just blinked at him instead.

"You're in the hospital. There was an accident. Do you remember, baby?"

I tried to shake my head no but even as I thought

that, I was remembering. I was remembering it all. I was a shape-shifter, a werewolf. My best friend, Pace, was dead and if it hadn't been for Corey my heart would have turned to stone. My mother had called the boy I loved, "this boy." She had said, "Think of the children." Rage had seized me. And I was bleeding and the moon was full. This was the combination that led to change. I had changed. My mother had seen a wolf in the garden. She didn't know that the wolf was me and she had shot at it. She had shot and there was a splintering pain in my left hand. My left hand . . . I couldn't take any more.

I had to close my eyes and sleep.

When I woke in the hospital again Dr. Nieberding was there.

"Corey!" I said. I tried to move. I looked down and saw the bandages wrapped around my hand. Some blood had stained the white. In my mind I saw my mother lift her gun. My hand. What had happened to my hand? I leaned forward and vomited over the side of the bed.

"Nurse," Nieberding called. He moved his chair closer to me. "Do you understand what's happened, Olivia?" he asked.

I stared at him. My eyes must have looked as wild as I felt because he cleared his throat and moved away slightly. There was the taste of acid in my mouth.

"You're in the hospital. There's been an accident. We don't know exactly what happened but we're looking into it."

"Corey!" I said. He was the only one I wanted, the only one who would understand. I tossed my head back and forth. Then I realized. My body was in restraints.

"We didn't want you to hurt yourself," Nieberding said. "When you're calmer we can take these off."

"Get away from me!" I could feel a stirring of the frenzy deep in my body. A month could have already passed since the last moon; I wasn't sure—I had lost all sense of time. I took a breath, trying to control it. I couldn't let it happen here. "Get me Corey!"

"Your mother wants you to know she is very concerned. She and your father are doing everything they can to find out how this happened."

I know how it happened.

"What did she tell you?" I growled.

"You had an argument and then you ran into the woods. A search party was sent out and they found you there . . . like this."

No! That was a lie. My mother had mistaken me for a wolf and shot me in our own backyard. I had run to the woods on three paws, leaving a trail of blood. A sound was starting in my throat, a low whistling hum that would escalate soon into something fierce and blood curdling.

The nurse came. "Visiting hours are over, Doctor," she said.

Nieberding stood up. "Yes, of course. And get this cleaned up, please." Wincing, he gestured to the vomit.

Dr. Nieberding walked away. I looked at the end of my arm. I thought of my left hand, how I had used it to pet dogs and cats, to care for them, to hand ice cream cones to people, to hold the handlebars of my bike, to stroke Corey's face. I retched again but there was nothing left in my stomach except bile.

The third time I woke up it was Corey again. My mother still hadn't come, at least not while I was conscious. It was night and the room was hushed and darkened. The air blew cool on my skin and my lips were parched.

I reached for his arm with my right hand and pulled Corey to me. By the soft light from the window I could see there were tears in his eyes.

"How could this have happened to me?" I sobbed.

He kissed my face. "It's going to be okay, baby."

"Okay?" I lifted my left arm. There was a fresh bandage on it now. "My hand! Corey! My hand."

"I know." He held me and we wept together, so

231

close that I couldn't tell whose breath I heard—mine or his.

I kept repeating, "What happened? What happened to me?"

"I'll be your hand," Corey said.

"But you're leaving me!"

"No, Liv. I'm not leaving. I'm not going to go anywhere without you."

"Where's my mom?" Suddenly, in spite of what she had done I felt like a little girl again, wanting her presence, the smell of her perfume and the feeling of her hands combing my hair.

But it was Corey who stroked my hair away from my forehead. "She's been here. Your dad came, too. They won't speak to me, though. I think they are trying to blame me for what happened. I wouldn't have gotten in at all if my mom didn't work here."

"Your mom knows?"

"She knows I've been camping in the waiting room and I won't go home without you."

"My hand," I sobbed again. "Corey!" How could I live like this, a monster without a hand?

"I know someone who can help," he said.

But I just wanted to sleep.

When I woke the next morning—I thought it was the next morning but it could have been longer—Joe Ranger was standing over me, holding a silver hand.

It looked just like the ones I'd seen in his shop but it gleamed—bright metal.

"What the hell is that?" I yelped.

"I brought you a present." His lips curled into a small, worried smile.

I remembered the newspaper articles in his room, the picture of me. I had trusted him once. "Get the fuck away!"

"Liv, this will help you."

"Yeah, right. Help. I asked you for help before. You want to kill me. I know what you are and what you did. And I'm not stupid. I know a little about myself. I know what silver is supposed to do to them, to . . . me."

"Calm down, Livvy. I thought you could do this on your own. You're getting there, mastering it, but this will make it easier. And it will protect you from your enemies."

"Get me Corey!"

Joe sat at my bedside, holding the strange metal object and I writhed away from him.

"You're not right about any of those things you said."

"What things? That you want to kill me? That you're a werewolf? That you're the full moon killer?" I made my voice loud on purpose.

"And you don't know how important you are to me or why," Joe went on, making his voice even quieter now.

For some reason I didn't scream. I guess I wanted to hear what he had to say and for some reason, as much as I was acting that way, I wasn't entirely afraid of Joe Ranger. "That's right. I don't know. How should I know? Why do you keep my picture in your drawer? I trusted you. You were one of the only people I trusted."

"Liv," he said. "I had a relationship with your mother before you were born. Do you understand?"

I looked at Joe. His hair was red like mine. His eyes were green like mine. He had watched over me since I could remember. Like a father.

"No!" I said. I'd heard enough. "Get him away!"

The nurse came in. I knew her. Corey's mom. "Core thought you'd be glad to see him." She looked hard at Joe. "I think you need to leave now, Mr. Ranger."

He stood up and shook his head sadly.

Then he put the silver hand down on the chair. And left.

It shone eerily and I wondered if it could hurt me. And, at the same time, I wanted it.

Joe Ranger was my father? My mother had slept with him? I tried to replay my whole life with this new knowledge. How my mother must have been so unhappy with my dad. I thought of them sleeping in their separate beds, hardly ever touching, never kissing. How my dad must have despised me because he knew on some level I wasn't his, but how he took care of me as his own anyway. I could see his suspicious glances, the way hate flared in his eyes when he drank too much and I did something that upset him. How Joe Ranger had watched over me because I was his child. How hard it must have been for my mom to look at me with my red hair and green eyes. How she must have grown to hate any wildness—mine, the wolves', Joe Ranger's—because it reminded her of her own, what she could never really have or be.

When Corey came back in I was crying again. "Baby?" He sat beside me. "I thought that would help. What happened?"

"Silver, Corey."

He glanced down at the thing on the chair. It was skillfully crafted. It looked just like my hand, as if Joe had used the hand that was gone as a model.

"Take it away!" I said.

Corey frowned so a crease formed between his eyebrows. "Didn't he explain it to you?"

"He's a freak, Corey. He's dangerous. I know what he did."

"Wait, what are you talking about?"

So I told Corey about the newspaper clippings in Joe's room and how he had seen me leaving his place. How I thought he was one, like me. How I believed Sasha had bitten him, cursed him that way. He was the full moon killer. I was sure. Actually, I wasn't sure I believed any of this but I needed to say it anyway, to distance Joe from me as much as possible. I didn't tell Corey the other part—that Joe had told me he was my father. I didn't want to say it out loud; it felt like too much to handle if I made it real with words.

Corey shook his head no. "Listen, Liv. They know who did it. It wasn't Joe."

"They know who did what?"

"There was another killing that night. The night you hurt your . . . The night this happened to you." He took my left arm and cradled it in his right, so gently. It was the first time he'd touched it. I didn't flinch. This was Corey. He had seen me change. He could handle everything, even this.

Then Corey told me about the off-duty police officers hunting in the woods; one, Jake Cunningham, had been killed and partially eaten that same night I'd frenzied. His friend had escaped and identified the murderer after spending the next night hunting for him in the woods with a posse of men.

This friend was not someone you mess with. This friend was the chief of police.

My father's friend Jake Cunningham was dead. My father had somehow found Sasha's cabin and now he had someone under arrest.

"He's been working on it nonstop. That's probably why he hasn't come here that much."

I wasn't sure if that was the only reason why my

father hadn't come. I was already a burden to him, a reminder of everything that had gone wrong. Now I was something worse—a reminder of the violence and pain that existed beneath the surface of our lives.

Corey took a newspaper out of his back pocket and showed me the picture. I recognized the light eyes, the thick dark hair with the thick sideburns and the lupine features.

"It looks like he killed them all, for the last four years. Olaf's dad, all of them."

"Victor," I said, remembering that night on the road after Carl Olaf had reached down my shirt. Victor had read my mind that night. I had felt him rummaging inside my head when we met on the road. He had heard me tell Sasha that my father had hit me in the face and he had growled low in his throat. I had dreamed of him in my room and I was never sure if it was actually a dream. My diary had been open on my nightstand. Scattered through it were the names Dale Tamblin, Sadie Nelson and Sherry Lee. I had thought at first that Joe Ranger had come into my room but it was Victor who had invaded my diary and my mind. He had said, "I am capable of many things. You could redeem me." I hadn't understood at the time. Was he talking of his ability to kill, and asking me to keep him from doing it again by taking him in my arms?

I thought of Victor standing in my room and my whole body went cold.

My father had even more reason to hate me now—I was, in part, the cause of his friend's death.

"Joe Ranger wants to help you," said Corey. He leaned in closer, whispering, "The hand will keep you from changing if you wear it."

He reached over and held it like something very precious, like the part of my body that was no longer there. I couldn't look away from what he held. But I couldn't take it, either. If I did, then I would be fully acknowledging that my hand was gone, that my mother had shot it off, that I would never have a human hand with five ingeniously human fingers, not ever again. I would die and my skeleton arm would end in a stump.

Also, if I took the hand, then I was fully accepting that Joe Ranger was more than a strange, kind man who had watched over me. He was the source of my mother's pain. He was my father.

I shuddered as I stared at the hand and then willed myself to look away from it. "Please, don't."

"Okay, baby," said Corey, stroking my head. "We'll get you out of here first and we will figure out what to do."

When my mother came to the hospital I didn't want her to comfort me the way I had imagined I would. She looked as if she had lost weight, her eyes were unfocused, as if she hadn't been sleeping and her hair—this was the part that freaked me out the most, because I'd never seen it like this before, at least not out of the house—was a mess. She asked how I was but we hardly talked about what had happened. We hardly talked about anything at all. She mentioned the full moon murders once, how great it was that my dad had solved the case, how he was the big hero now. She also started to talk about things she was going to order from catalogs but I stopped her, saying I was feeling sick, and eventually she left.

After one of these visits I called Corey and he came right over. He brought some wildflowers he had picked along the way and put them in an old apple juice bottle by my bed.

"I need a plan now," I said, after I had thanked him for the flowers. "I can't go home with her."

He nodded. "I know. I've been thinking about it."

"But you're about to leave for school."

"I told you, Liv, I'm not going anywhere without you."

"We can't stay in this town," I said. "It's not even safe for us. I don't know what Victor's brothers will do now that he's in prison."

"And your dad put him there. Believe me, I've been

thinking about it." Corey stroked my hair. "I'm going to take you with me. As soon as they release you I'm going to come get you and we'll go."

"Where?"

"East," Corey told me. "Where the sun rises. Like we always planned."

I reached out for him and he leaned over and kissed my mouth. A warmth tingled through my body. I reached up with my left hand to touch Corey's unshaven face, forgetting that there was nothing at the end of my arm. No hand, no miracle of fingers with their dexterity and sensitivity to sensations of hot and cold, smooth and rough. Tears again. It seemed like I was always crying now. Damn. I thought about the silver hand, so delicately crafted that it looked like something that could have been in a museum. Maybe I would let Corey strap it to my ruined stump. Maybe Corey and I still had a chance to be free.

As if he could read my mind, Corey said, "The first night you're home, at midnight, I'll come for you.

I'll bring it with me." He didn't say "the silver hand" but I knew that was what he meant.

My mother and father (the man I had always believed was my father, the one who looked nothing like me) finally brought me home. When we got home, that cool afternoon in September, as the students were arriving for school and the air smelled of wood smoke and dried leaves, all the TVs were on and my gramp was dozing in front of the big one in the living room. I looked around at the house full of television sets. Liquor bottles gleamed in the cabinets. The refrigerator was full of meat. Gossip magazines and catalogs were piled on all the tables. And everything was clean.

It all seemed perfectly normal. Happy America. Except that I was a werewolf, my mother had shot off my hand and one of my father's men had been brutally murdered. But no one would talk about it.

"I've ordered you some cute new jeans and things for when school starts," my mother said, holding up a catalog. I glared at her.

"Cindy," my dad said. "Not now."

She looked at him, surprised. "What, Jeff? She needs clothes."

My dad turned off the TV in front of Gramp. He stirred in his chair and made a wheezing sound.

"Just not now." My dad went to pour himself a scotch. Then stopped and turned to me. "Do you need anything, Olivia?"

I shook my head. Gramp opened his eyes. "Olivia!" he said. "You're home." He lifted himself from his chair with effort.

I went to meet him, trying to hide my stump as best I could. He had tears in his eyes. I put my arms around him. He'd wanted to visit me in the hospital but they hadn't let him.

"I'm sorry," I said.

"It's not your fault. None of it was your fault. Remember that. Live responsibly but without guilt for what is past." He let go of my shoulders and gripped my right hand in both of his. "You must try, Olivia."

"Liv, why don't you go upstairs and lie down," said my mom. "I'll bring you some food and a magazine."

"I hate your magazines," I said. "I hate your food."

She brushed invisible lint off her shirt and went to the refrigerator. "I know you've been through a lot but that's no reason to speak to me like that."

"Mom," I said. "'Been through a lot'? My hand got shot off. Do you see this?" I held up the stump, still wrapped in a bandage.

"Jeff . . . ," my mom said.

"You shot me." I was shouting now. "You shot off my hand!"

"Jeff," my mom said again. Her eyes were huge and she took a step away from me as if I were a crazed monster. I realized she didn't know. Either she really didn't know or she had blocked it from her mind, the way I had blocked the clues to what I was for so many years. But I remembered how she had called my name before she shot me, how she had glanced back at my window as if she was wondering if I was in there or if, maybe, this creature before her, so like the two wolves she had shot before, was me. She didn't know for sure if she had shot me but there was doubt in her mind. I didn't hate her for the doubt; I hated her for not acknowledging it, for blocking out everything except what she wanted to believe.

My dad walked over to me. He hadn't touched me in years except to hit me. I backed away. I could feel my blood heating up. The moon would rise tonight.

"Liv," he said. "Olivia."

"You're not much different," I told him. My voice was soft and I hung my head. "When you get mad and you get drunk and you hit me in the face."

My dad cleared his throat. "I'm sorry," he said.

My mom came over and touched his arm. He brushed her away. "Olivia, I don't understand what is happening but I see you are hurt. And it's not okay. And I'm going to find out who did this to you."

He didn't know anything, that was for sure, but

maybe part of him sensed something because he had never sounded this sympathetic. I looked at him. His face was red. He had folds under his eyes. He had raised me as his own but it was clear I never was. I looked at my mom with her pleading face. *Part of her knows*, I thought again. *Part of her knows what she did.* But I wasn't going to tell him, confirm his suspicions and bring more pain on them. It was enough; we'd all had enough.

"No one did this to me," I said. "I did this to myself."

Scoot began to bark hysterically.

"What's that in the yard?" Gramp pointed. "Out in the yard! Lookit!"

We turned and saw a shadow slip behind a tree.

"A wolf!" Gramp said. "I'll be damned if it wasn't one."

My mom ran toward the window but she crashed into the glass coffee table and slumped to the ground. Her shin was bleeding. A bright red trickle. I inadvertently touched my top lip with my tongue.

My mom looked from me to my dad and back, then to Gramp, then to Dad again. "Isn't anyone going to ask if I'm okay?" She paused. "I guess not. Because I always say everything is okay. But you know what? I have some news for all of you. I am not okay." She looked at me. "I loved you. I did everything for you. I'm a good mother. But you're right. Nothing is okay and it won't ever be."

Then she started to cry. Maybe, someday, she would be strong enough to acknowledge what she had done. But I wouldn't be there to see it.

The shadow in the garden was gone. I backed away from my mother. Then I turned. I ran upstairs and packed a backpack and sat by the window. My right hand was shaking so much it seemed like it belonged to someone else. My other hand was still because it wasn't there.

May love's fire burn away my pain.

Corey came at midnight as we had planned. I was lying on the floor breathing as deeply as I could—even though the breath kept catching in my chest—trying to keep the change from coming on. He knelt beside me and I noticed the hair on his cheeks and chin; he'd never had so much before. He looked a lot older to me then.

"My mom said the bandages can come off now."

I flinched.

"May I?

Corey was used to handling fragile, sick animals. Once he'd cared for a sick lamb. He kept it in a box in his room and fed it with a dropper. When it died he buried it in his garden.

I let Corey unwrap the bandages. My head was turned away but when I felt his touch on my wrist— so gentle—I looked back. My arm seemed smaller and paler as if it had shrunk. As if it wasn't my arm at all but the arm of a small child. But not a normal child. It ended in a roughly tapered stump.

Corey slipped the silver hand over my wrist. It attached with a delicate strap above my elbow.

I waited for something to happen. For me to die,

maybe. For more pain. But there was nothing, only a feeling of calm. And Corey was holding my hand again, the way he used to hold my hand of bone and flesh.

He helped me up and took my backpack.

We climbed down into the garden.

"How are we getting there?" I asked him. I hadn't even thought of it.

"I have something to show you," Corey said, heading for the road.

Then, out of the shadows came the six figures. Their eyes were golden mirrors. They were brothers. Wolves.

I heard them though they did not speak in words.

Victor has been sacrificed.

All those killings—he was trying to protect you!

He thought you were his chosen bride, because he had never met a female like us before.

But you are nothing compared to him.

Bitch.

This is the third generation of our family that your family has taken.

Soon we will have our revenge.

Part of me had dreamed of a life with these men and their mother, deep in the forest where no one could find us. I would be the bride of the most handsome and most brutal of them all. I could live true to my animal nature, let the beast inside me come out whenever she wished, without having to wear a piece of metal to control her. But just as I was not my mother with her fear, I was not Sasha with her brutality. I would have to find who I was, and whoever that was lived somewhere between them. Nor was I a bride for Victor, who had taken my breath away in the shadows of my room and who had also killed all those men, men whose children (or, in the last case, whose friend) had hurt me in some way.

I lifted my silver hand in the moonlight and the six brothers lowered their heads to the ground, whining. So it affected them differently, my silver hand.

We were different. I would have been relieved at this proof that I was perhaps more human than monster. But their eyes were fixed on Corey.

He's ours, they said. *If you won't be,* sister. *Our brother showed you compassion. He is gone. We are here now.*

Corey squeezed my right hand so hard that it hurt. Victor was in prison and my father had put him there. I wore a silver hand but Corey had nothing to protect him, not even me anymore now that Victor was gone.

But Corey wasn't asking me to protect him.

He was different now.

Corey's eyes flashed. The hair on his face made him look a lot tougher. A sound stirred from his throat like the voice of the night.

A month ago, when Victor cornered us in the woods Corey had hidden behind me. But he had changed. Now he frightened me but he was also beautiful in his strength. He was everything I wanted and maybe he was different partly because of me. And it was going to be my fault when he attacked the six wolves that surrounded us and they tore him to shreds of flesh and blood.

"Corey!" I shouted. I moved toward him but he didn't seem to hear or see me. He stepped closer to the wolves. "Corey, no!"

And then Joe Ranger was there.

He stood at the edge of the garden, wearing a plaid flannel shirt, his gun cocked on his shoulder and his eyes narrow slits. "Silver bullets, boys," Joe said. "And it is time to leave." Then, out of the corner of his mouth, he added, "You, too, kids." And with his free hand he shooed us off.

Corey reached out and took the silver hand my real father had made for me in his own warm hand.

I looked back at Joe. He was standing his ground and the wolves slunk away. His eyes met mine.

"Be safe, my girl."

Then he left, too. I watched my father become part of the trees along the gulley. My chest tightened as I realized I might never see him again. But I had ways to remember him; I had Joe Ranger's red hair, his green eyes and his silver hand.

"Come on," Corey said, bringing me back to him.

"Where are we going? How?"

"You'll see."

We were running along the road out of town but in another way I was running back through my life. Here was me lying in the hospital with Corey and Joe Ranger at my side. I looked into Joe's eyes and saw where I had come from, the pain and also the beauty. I looked into Corey's eyes and saw where I was going, the trepidation and the excitement. Here was me bleeding in the woods, bleeding from my ruined hand, the victim of my mother's gunshot. Here was my mother fallen, weeping on the yellow linoleum tiles of the kitchen floor. She had not meant to hurt her daughter and destroy her family. She had been hurt, too, as she ran from her own pain, her own wild nature. Here was my father, so upright and respected by day, drinking by night, swallowing his betrayal and his rage in angry mouthfuls, sleeping in his twin bed. Here was my gentle grandfather who had not seen the destruction he caused in my mother's life, calling her mother an angel and taking his daughter up in a helicopter to shoot wolves that showed up better against the white landscape. Here was Pace hanging from a rope in his closet, just like Michael Fairborn did long ago. Here was Pace dancing with me. Here was Victor, kneeling on my carpet, spreading roses on the bed. Here was Victor ripping the carcasses to shreds with his teeth. Here was Corey making love to me in the woods while our eyes sparkled with the light of a thousand fireflies. Here was Sasha with blood on her paws from the meat she had killed for me. Here was her husband and her father killed by my mother's hand. Here was Corey and Pace and me exploring the ruins of buildings where ghosts mourned their unfinished lives. Here was me changing into something I had not understood, something with hair and teeth and hunger and ferocity and power. Here was me as a baby, sleeping peacefully in my mother's arms while she dreamed of her wild lover who would never come back to her bed. Here was my mother in a helicopter, taking aim.

Corey led me to the shiny black motorcycle parked in the shadows at the side of the road.

"She's ours," he said, getting on. "Liv, meet Lupe, Lupe, Liv. She'll take us all the way."

I slung my thigh over the black leather seat and got on behind him. The engine revved and roared like a beast as we took off into the night. Wind grabbed at my hair, flaring red strands around us. I held on tight to Corey's waist and I could smell his sweat—a scent of adventure and hope and love.

"How did you get this?" I shouted over the wind.

"I saved up for her all summer."

"Your school money?"

"We'll figure it out."

On the way out of town I asked him to stop at the house on Green Street. Behind the wall of Christmas trees we could see the sharply peaked roof and the front parlor window. This time, two lights burned inside. Maybe they were fireflies. Or maybe not.

"Good-bye, Pace," I said as we rode away.

I reached around Corey's waist and placed my silver hand over his heart. It beat in perfect rhythm with my own. I no longer wondered who I was. I knew.

FRANCESCA LIA BLOCK, winner of the prestigious Margaret A. Edwards Award, is the author of many acclaimed and bestselling books, including *Weetzie Bat, Dangerous Angels: The Weetzie Bat Books,* the collection of stories *Blood Roses,* the poetry collection *How to (Un)cage a Girl,* the novel *The Waters & the Wild,* the illustrated novella *House of Dolls,* and the gothic vampire romance *Pretty Dead.* Her work is published around the world. You can visit her online at www.francescaliablock.com.